DREAMS IN HER HEAD

CLARE C. MARSHALL

For Kerry

Enjoy!

BOOK TWO
THE SPARKSTONE SAGA

Editing: Rachel Small
Cover Illustration: Bramasta Aji
Cover Design: David Farrell

FAERY INK PRESS
faeryinkpress.com
Calgary, Alberta
clare@faeryinkpress.com

Other books by Clare C. Marshall:

Stars In Her Eyes (Sparkstone Saga #1)
The Violet Fox (The Violet Fox Series #1)
Within

PART ONE

A dream is a window, dear scribe. One only needs to crawl far enough inside to advance into another world.

—J.G.C., from *Campbell's Multiple Verses*

PROLOGUE

If there is one thing I am sure of in this moment, it is this: there is a door somewhere nearby, and soon, Sunni will ask me to open it.

Tonight we are not in Rogers Hall at Sparkstone University. That is usually where the dreams take place. Tonight, Sunni and I stroll through a labyrinth of bookshelves in an impossibly large room. Above us is a glass ceiling that glows supernaturally green, as if we are in the City of Oz.

Sunni walks behind me, and I steal a glance at her. In the back of my mind, a small voice whispers that she is not really Sunni. Sunni is dead, and her body has been dissected to further the Collective's technological research, to advance its evil agenda, whatever it may be. Yet tonight, she is a phoenix stepping from fiery ashes, reborn. The light filtering in from the ceiling, although green, bathes Sunni's blonde curls in orange and red hues and creates colourful shadows on her white T-shirt and pants.

She thumbs the rows of books on the wooden shelves as we pass. "So many worlds."

Her Texan twang echoes through the large library, and pink and green ribbons flow from her lips and intertwine like a double helix. They are physical manifestations of my synesthesia, because that is possible here.

We're still at Sparkstone, aren't we. I don't have to open my mouth to talk here. Telepathy is much easier, much faster. I understand why our friend Wil prefers it. I wish I had that power in real life.

"Yes, still at Sparkstone. Deep underground, though," Sunni tells me. I don't know why Sunni doesn't speak with her mind. She probably could if she wanted to, but I prefer her acting as she was when she was alive.

She lets her hand fall lazily to her side. As it falls, I notice for the first time that the shelves have words carved into them. Squinting, I focus my razor-sharp vision until the words become clear: *Saturday, September 13. Saturday, September 13.* It repeats everywhere.

"That's the day this place gets torn down," Sunni says. "They don't need it no more."

They meaning the Collective, the alien organization that runs Sparkstone University and god knows what else on Earth.

Why don't they need it?

"Oh, they're getting ready for phase four or five, I reckon."

And what does that mean?

Instead of answering, Sunni wraps her hand around my wrist and pulls us to a standstill. The aisle of shelving we're walking down seems to stretch like an elastic band. I'm in the middle of the *Vertigo* effect you see in movies— things look as if they're moving away, even though they're not. Wings flutter somewhere in the distance. No, not wings. It's the sound of a thousand pages flipping all at once.

"Duck," Sunni whispers.

I do, but she doesn't let go. Dozens of bookshelves are ripped from the floor, but I do not feel the breeze as they fly over our heads and crash somewhere behind us. A tornado of books rises before us and dissipates just as quickly to make room for a new resident: a giant pale-blue eye.

As the eye flickers in an invisible socket, scanning what's left of the library at supernatural speed, it creates gusts of wind that almost knock me off my feet. Sunni remains steadfast, unmoving in the face of this faceless eye, returning its unblinking stare without fear.

What is that? I ask her.

"Campbell," she replies simply.

The word lights up my brain. Joseph G. Campbell is whom I'm searching for, whom Sunni was searching for, before the Collective killed her. He has something to do with its agenda—whether he works for the Collective or against it, I'm not sure. His powers seem to be far-reaching, and he himself seems always just out of reach.

As I stare into the abnormally large eye of the one who could help or harm me, Sunni places a firm hand on my lower back and pushes me closer. "Go through."

I frown, and in this place, my face is heavy—possibly because I am actually frowning in the real world. *What? Why? How?*

"Go *through*, Ingrid."

It's an eye. How do I go—?

The question is answered when streams of white light slice through the large black pupil—a vertical cut, then two horizontal cuts at ninety-degree angles—creating a door.

Sunni's voice grows louder, more ethereal. "Open the door, Ingrid."

I turn to face her, but Sunni is gone. She has morphed into our greatest enemy: Jadore. The humanoid reptilian seductress stands before me, staring at me with reflective black eyes, her dark dress rippling around her legs. Her teeth are sharp points, and blood drips from her mouth, as if she's just fed on someone. Sunni, probably, as Jadore was the one who ended Sunni's life in the real world.

The small voice in the back of my mind whispers that this isn't real, that Jadore would never show her true face anywhere at Sparkstone in the light of day. But the voice also whispers that I am safe in my bed on the third floor of Rita House, and while this is true, I know that I will never be safe again.

The wind whistles and blows stronger as Jadore tackles me to the floor. She rakes her sharp nails across the top of my head and tries to dig through my hair, through my skull. She wants my brain. I resist but she's so strong. I'm not like my new friends—I can't control the power I have, not yet. It's too soon.

Powerful searing light blasts over us. The door in the pupil. It's opening wider. But I can't get near it, not with Jadore on top of me. She has cracked my skull and is reaching inside my head. Obscuring my view.

Now I'm watching from outside myself. I'm someone else, but I'm still tethered to my body with an invisible rope. Jadore feeds on me enthusiastically. My gaze strays to Campbell's eye. In the threshold of the pupil door, there is a silhouette of a man. Although the form is familiar, it is presented as an empty space that my brain can't yet fill.

Joseph G. Campbell: a shadow in the realm of the forever sun.

∽

...wind through the thicket...
...breathe in the darkness...
...become its master...
...Ingrid, open the door.

My legs are so twisted in the blankets and I'm in such need to get out of bed that I fall to the floor in a confused, sweaty heap. I can't remember where I am. Or what's real.

Breathe in. Breathe out. Carpet. It smells new. That's because it is new. This room is old, but everything in it, including me, is new. And I finally remember: I'm at Sparkstone University. In my new dorm room in Rita House. Sunni's old room. Stripped of everything that was Sunni by the aliens in disguise, it was remade and redecorated for me, as it was the first room to become available in the girls' residences.

I lie on the floor until my breathing becomes more normal. This is the third time this week I've had a dream like that, where I'm with Sunni again, and there's a door before me, and Jadore shows up and kills me. It sounds silly when I explain it to myself when I'm awake, and the feeling of immediate danger has faded. But I know better than to ignore the dream. It's a warning.

My cell phone sits on my nightstand, beside my alarm clock. I retrieve the phone with a sleepy grip and confirm the date. September eighth. Monday morning.

The dream was specific in a way it hasn't been before, giving me a date. Saturday, September thirteenth. I wonder what it means.

Untangling my limbs, I sit up and lean against the bed. My matted long red hair hangs free around my shoulders. The whispers at the end of the dream were so real. Audio hallucinations are sometimes common after intense dreams—I'd read that somewhere somewhat credible. I know the voice. I'd only known Sunniva Harris for a day, but her face and her sound are ingrained in my memory.

Somehow, she's speaking to me in my dreams. She's trying to send me a message.

I hug my pillow to my chest and stare at the framed photo on my nightstand. It's of me, Mum, and Dad, taken last summer on a vacation in Cape Breton, Nova Scotia. Some nice tourist took it for us. We're in front of a tree at the Alexander Graham Bell Museum, and behind us, a sailboat leaves a rippling trail. My mom is squinting because the sun is in her eyes, but my dad is grinning, and I've got my arms around them both. Craig and Margaret Stanley. I wish I were with them now.

I press the cool glass of the frame against my sweaty forehead. I don't want to be here. I didn't ask to be in this place, with these extraterrestrial problems. I want Sunni to be alive again. I want to see my parents, and have them tell me that it's okay.

But more than anything else, I want to go home.

CHAPTER 1

"Ace of clubs, suckers," Misty says, sneering.

With a satisfied look on her face, she tosses the card onto the reject pile. I look down at my hand. I have four cards left and could definitely win. But it's not my turn. It's Jia's, since she's sitting directly across from Misty. Then it's Wil's turn, and then mine.

Jia is concentrating hard, but her expression does not reveal it. Calm and collected, she is. Only her almond-shaped eyes reveal a competitive, fierce spirit. She plays a two of spades and shoots Wil a triumphant look.

Wil barely glances at his hand as he picks up two cards and then plays a five of spades. He adjusts his glasses as he stares out the window of the Evergreen Café. Two white trucks drive down the main road—Sparkstone Boulevard—then turn off onto a side road and make their way towards the research labs at the edge of the town of Sparkstone. His dark eyes follow them intently.

Playing cards keeps our hands busy. More than that, it helps us temporarily forget the terrible responsibilities weighing on us—such as our mission to bring down the Collective.

The distraction also helps us deal with Sunni's death.

I play a seven of spades, and then Misty plays a Joker, sending Jia into a huff. Wil throws out his own Joker, which delights Misty, as she only has one card left. She plays a seven of hearts and throws up her hands in victory.

"Playin' real good today," Misty says, smirking. Her smiles are rare. She and Sunni had been close, Jia told me—friends before they came to Sparkstone.

"For someone who knows a bunch of languages, your English isn't that great," I remark.

Misty gives me a look I've come to know well in the past week that I've hung out with the Sparks: narrowed eyes, thick with black mascara, and drawn, almost snarling lips that forbid joy. The look is accompanied by a light snort that suggests I am the dumbest person at the table.

"Just because I speak ten languages good don't mean I have to speak them *well*," she replies, flinging the reject cards at Jia, who is collecting the deck.

It's easy to underestimate Misty, to take her at face value as a messed up, angry girl who has several facial piercings, dresses in dark clothes, and stares at you as though she's got a death wish. I try not to misjudge her; I try not to engage in her attempts to rile me. Arguing with her is like trying to move a wall by snapping your fingers, so I just shrug.

A waitress trudges by, tall and lithe but wearing clunky high heels that *clomp-clomp* on the tile. She leaves the cheque on the table between Wil and me.

Jia smiles and bows her head in victory to Misty, then nudges Wil playfully. "Someone over here needs to pay more attention to his cards."

Wil's dark skin flushes red momentarily, and he adjusts his round wire-framed glasses, like this will help him manage his embarrassment. He glances at his watch. "That's the last round. We should pay up. Bill is"—he picks up the cheque—"thirty-five, plus tip. Which is, uh ... "

He stutters only for a second, but Misty rips into him. "Your IQ is three standard deviations above the mean and you can't figure out tip?" She snickers again.

"Hey, hey, I'm distracted." His eyes flicker to the corners of the room, where hidden cameras are apt to live.

Everyone in the small northern Alberta town of Sparkstone is watched because the Collective harvests students with an active Gene 213 in their body. Supposedly this gene activates superpowers in humans and manifests itself in many different ways. It allows Wil to manipulate technology, communicate telepathically, and feel people's emotions and presence.

My gaze sweeps the room. Sure enough, there's a tiny red light in the upper right corner, just above the chalkboard menu on the wall, and the counter where we ordered our food. Wil could block the camera's audio and video, but we're trying to limit the use of his powers. Today, I imagine he's concentrating on keeping the camera's gaze focused on everything but us so as not to arouse Professor Jadore's suspicion.

Even thinking about her name brings up twisted images of her reptilian face and soulless black eyes from my nightmares. We have to pretend she didn't kill Sunni a week ago while we sit in her tutorial and she continues to masquerade as a blind human professor.

We are all dreading our tutorial with her this morning even more than usual. In the week since Sunni's murder,

Misty, Jia, and Wil have not been productive with respect to their projects. Sparkstone University is different from other undergraduate schools in that instead of classes and exams, we have tutorials and personal projects that professors oversee. The projects are supposed to relate to the two majors we choose, and usually they require a lot of individual research. We are expected to explore a topic in a new and interesting way. Wil has finished his project for the semester, but he's struggling to come up with a new one and is starting to run out of technical mumbo-jumbo to feed Jadore. My concentration hasn't been much better.

"You know—"

Wil holds up a hand to cut Misty off. "I know what you're going to say. And it's not a good idea."

Misty snarls. She hates it when Wil can predict her arguments. I don't care much for it either. "You're not the only one at the table, jackass."

"Fine. But it's not a good idea."

Jia looks back and forth between the two of them. "What?"

Misty's mouth twists as she cracks a few knuckles. "We should call her mother and tell her what really happened."

We don't have to ask who *her* is. Sunni. But I'm surprised. Jia, Wil, and I try not to bring up Sunni while Misty is around. Misty had gone insane on the day Sunni was murdered. This is the first time she's dared to say her name out loud since.

"How would that help us at all? And would she believe it?" I ask.

Shrugging, Misty leans back in the booth. "Didn't say it would help, or that she'd believe us. Just sayin' that she deserves to know the truth."

I muse on this. If I died here, I'd want my parents to know the truth. But it would take a lot of explaining to get them to believe that some people have superpowers and that aliens are harvesting our genes.

"We should do nothing, for now," Wil says. He switches to telepathy. *No doubt the Collective has contacted Sunni's mother and told her that Sunni has been transferred. I think it's only a matter of time before Mrs. Harris figures out that something is wrong.*

I want to believe this is true, but somehow I doubt that the Collective would massively screw that up. Who knows how many young adults the aliens have captured and murdered, just for their genes. Their influence is far-reaching—and the hafelglob, one of the many alien races of the Collective, could even be using their shape-shifting abilities to impersonate students who have been killed.

I shiver. Sunni's kind-hearted, brave spirit, replaced with gross alien slime. It just isn't fair. Nothing is fair anymore.

My cell phone buzzes in my jean-skirt pocket. I nearly jump out of my seat. Jia gives me a worried look but I reassure her with a smile as I dig out the phone. The phone number is Dad's cell, and my smile becomes a grin.

"Hi, Dad!"

"Hey!" The reception isn't great, and it sounds like he's in a busy place. "Did I catch you at a bad time? You're not studying or anything, are you?"

"No, just…hanging out with friends." I glance around the table at my mishmash of new peers and then rise from the table and walk to the other side of the café.

"That's great. So you're getting along, then, with your classes?"

"No classes here, Dad, remember? Tutorials and independent projects." I've talked to him maybe once since he and Mum dropped me off over a week ago.

"Well, I hope you're not spending too much time having fun. With friends, I mean. What is your project about again?"

I roll my eyes. "Dad! I don't want to waste all my cell phone minutes telling you about my boring school stuff. Tell me about you and Mum. You guys are all right, right?"

He chuckles. "Yes, yes, we're fine. We're supposed to be the ones worrying about you, not the other way around! You know...your mother misses you a lot. I miss you a lot." There's a moment of tender silence on his end. "You know, if your *boring school stuff* is too complicated for your old man, you just say so. I won't get offended."

"No, Dad. It's...it's not too complicated for you." My dad is a pretty smart guy. "It's just stuff to do with the brain and how it reacts to...um...external stimuli."

"Oooh. You going to dissect someone's brain over there?"

My gut clinches. The joke is too soon. "No."

"Okay, okay, just kidding." There's some noise on the other end, and a lot of static, and I hear Dad talking to someone else. Then: "Listen, Ingrid, I have to go. Just thought I'd give you a call to see how you were doing. I'm glad to hear you're all settled in."

"Yeah." I swallow. My throat is tight. "I miss you a lot, Dad."

"I know. We miss you too. Love you! Talk to you again soon."

"Bye, Dad."

I wait for him to hang up. The click in my ear is one of the worst sounds I've ever heard. I hate having my parents so far away. The three of us—Mum, Dad, and I—we're a close family, and it was only a few days ago that Jadore threatened the safety of everyone I loved if I tried to do anything rash against the Collective. She doesn't know that I somehow magically teleported from an exploding ship to Earth. That the important powers supposedly inside me, powers needed to defend our world, had awakened—if only briefly.

I return to the table and sit next to Misty. "All right, let's get out of here. We'll get together later. For lunch."

Jia shifts and reaches into her purse for her wallet. She radiates a sense of calm, as if nothing paranormal is happening around her, and I wish I could do the same. A purple ten appears between her fingers, and she lays it on the table. Wil pulls out a twenty from his wallet, and Misty grimaces then nods a reluctant thanks.

I gulp and dig through my own purse. Thankfully, I'm not short. I slap down a ten dollar bill and do some quick mental math. I've spent at least sixty dollars on food in the past couple of days. I think I have fifty dollars left in cash, and then I'll be burning through what little I have in my savings account, via my debit card. Avoiding the cafeteria is expensive. And I'm not sure if it's doing me any good. My stomach has been topsy-turvy these past few days, but it's just nerves. I haven't thrown up since my first day at Sparkstone, when the cafeteria food practically seduced me into eating it and turned me into a mind-controlled freak. Whatever poison they put in the food is effective, and we avoid it like the plague.

Scooting out of the booth, Wil waves to the server. Jia

gets out after him. "Hey, Ingrid, do you want to go for a run with me later?"

Exercise and I don't generally mix, but Jia is good company, and I know that fighting aliens will be easier once I'm in shape. "Sure. This evening, maybe?"

"Or after tutorial." A small smile spreads across her face. She's not going to let me escape this time. I said no to her yesterday.

"Okay, okay."

Misty nudges me and I slide out, freeing her. She massages her arms and looks warily out the large windows. I follow her gaze, and goosebumps blaze a hellish cold trail up my arms and down my back.

A man wearing blue maintenance-worker overalls and a navy baseball cap is standing across the road, staring at us through the window. But he's not really a man. Beneath that human image is a mess of tentacles and a spiralling, deadly garden of teeth in a hideous, drooling mouth. It's Ohz, the hafelglob, and I know from his smug smile that he's waiting for me.

Wil sees him too. My friend hovers nearby, silently waiting for me to decide how to handle the alien. Taking a deep breath, I put on my game face and march towards the door. I won't let the alien see how terrified I am. I won't.

Beside me, Jia pushes the door open and whispers in my ear. "You say the word, and we can be gone. We don't have to deal with him."

I nod. "Thanks, Jia. But I can't hide forever."

Technically, we could hide, as Jia has the power to turn herself and anything she touches invisible. But it would only delay the inevitable, not to mention make the Collective incredibly suspicious.

We step onto the patio, then walk down the stairs to the sidewalk. Ohz ambles across the road, hands in his pockets. There are three cars coming towards him but he pays the vehicles no mind. They slow for him, and someone honks a horn, but he is not afraid of traffic. I grit my teeth as his boots claim our side of the road just a few feet in front of us.

"We're going to be late for tutorial," Misty grumbles.

She's right. And we can't afford to have Jadore breathing down our necks even more than she already is. I avoid eye contact with Ohz and start down the sidewalk, towards Sparkstone campus.

"Ingrid Stanley," Ohz says, in his strange Indian-German-Italian hybrid accent. "Will she not stop to talk with me, miss?"

Misty, Jia, and Wil form a human wall around me and keep pace as I tear down the sidewalk past the alien in disguise. MacLeod Hall is a five-minute walk away, and if we hurry, we can make it to tutorial on time.

"Has information, Ohz does." He smacks his lips together.

Misty swivels around. "Stay away." Her palms glow a bright red. "Or else."

Now I chance a glance at him. Ohz looks Misty up and down, evaluating her strength. Misty singlehandedly took some hafelglob down during our last encounter. No doubt Ohz remembers that. The creepy smile slides off his face.

"This one not hurt the *Crosskey*," he replies, his voice quieting at the word *Crosskey*. He throws me a fervent look. I still haven't figured out why he calls me this. He holds up his hands, as if to surrender. "But Crosskey hurt Ohz. Deeply. You not remember?"

Of course I remember. I rammed the blunt end of a broom handle into his shifting form, and puss exploded all over my temporary room. And my clothes. And my boots. It had taken me hours to scrub all that alien scum off my precious leather boots.

"We don't want any trouble," I say. "We're going to be late for tutorial."

"Mmm. Don't want Mistress mad. No, Crosskey, no." He slows his pace, and sticks his tongue out. "Warning, then. Not in a good mood, Mistress. Think she not notice you skipping cafeteria? You think café food any better? Café is open before noon now. Think this is a coincidence? Crosskey, think twice!"

He's shouting now, and my stomach lurches. I exchange a worried look with Wil. My hurried pace turns into a run. No, no, no. Curse this damn school and all the aliens in it. Jia and Wil stay with me, but Misty runs on ahead.

I considered this, Wil says to our minds. *But I don't know how we can avoid ingesting whatever poison is in the food. If the alien is telling the truth, no doubt Jadore will infect all food in the town. We may have to grow our own. But that would be Sunni's domain…*

Misty throws a deadly glare back at us for bringing up Sunni, and then sprints away. She grows smaller and smaller on the grassy plains.

"Growing food takes time," Jia says between even breaths. "We need more information about whatever it is they're putting in the food so we can…can stop it."

Easier said than done. The Collective could pump drugs into any food made in this town. Fortunately none of us have felt ill yet from eating at the Evergreen Café, but as Wil said, maybe it's only a matter of time.

And time is something we don't have this morning. I check my cell phone. Three minutes past the hour. Dammit. Late already. And my side is cramping. Wil and Jia are more fit than I am, so I wave for them to go ahead. Wil raises an *are you sure* eyebrow, and I nod. There's no need for Jadore to be angry at all of us.

I slow my pace, clutching my side, and it takes me another five minutes to get to MacLeod Hall. The hallways are almost empty, save a couple of stragglers collecting items from the lockers that line the right wall, between the classroom doors. Room 216, that's me. The door is closed and a shadow moves within. Jadore's shadow. She's standing with her back to the door, leaning on her cane.

I can do this. I've done some research. Just spit it out at her, and you will have survived another day.

I roll my eyes at my thoughts as I venture towards my locker. Survive. Because that's all I feel I can do right now. The school is dangling on the edge of an alien invasion, but my hands are tied. My shaking fingers twist the combination lock. Another minute goes by. Another minute I'm late, another minute's worth of Jadore's wrath washing over me. But I can take it. I have to. I can do this.

I draw in a breath of strength as the lock clicks and I swing the door open. Then I take a step back, blinking in surprise. My backpack is in the locker, of course, but so are at least ten black artist's tubes. Ethan's artwork. Even seeing his things makes my heart go pitter-patter. We are sharing a locker, and a romantic tension that is hard to deny. Whenever he's around, it's hard for me to keep it together, and I'm having a hard enough time as it is keeping it together—especially since the morning he found me lying in the grass field beside the campus. I made a total fool out of myself and kissed him goodbye because I thought I was dead.

No time to think about silly, embarrassing moments. I have to prepare for Jadore. I maneuver my backpack around Ethan's art tubes and swing it over my shoulder, then shut the locker door.

"Oh, hold that, don't close it."

My heart leaps into my throat, and I almost gag I'm so caught off guard by my new favourite British voice. I hadn't even heard him approach. Now he's here, in the flesh, and my skin shivers hot and cold.

I turn and step awkwardly, slowly, to the side, so I can feel the warmth of his body as he reaches over me to reopen the locker door. His dark hair is ruffled, his clothes need an iron, and his fingers are permanently stained black from his charcoal, but somehow all of these elements add up to nothing short of handsome.

I cross my arms. I should really be going. Yet, here I am. Not going. And we're all alone in the hallway.

"You all right? Haven't really seen you much lately," Ethan says as he pulls out some tubes and tucks them under his arm.

"Uh-huh. Um, I mean, yeah I'm doing pretty good." So, so dumb. I'm getting nervous now. "How have you been?"

"Oh, you know. Holed up in my studio. Professor Jensen loves to smother me in smaller assignments. Really pushes me, wants me to create a larger body of work. I think I might be exhibiting in a few months. Not really sure where though. There aren't many art galleries here in Sparkstone. Calgary, maybe?"

"That's great! I'm sure any gallery would love to have some of your stuff to exhibit. Not that I know anything about that, or anything. And…and not to say that my praise means nothing. Because it's…sincere."

He chuckles at my nervous ranting. He's juggling some of the tubes, so I help him close the locker.

"So you taking those to your tutorial now?" I ask.

"Yeah, in like five or ten minutes or something." He frowns. "Don't you have tutorial right now? Jadore'll be bloody mad at you if you're supposed to be in there and you're not."

My eyes dart towards the door. I am way past late. Maybe I just shouldn't go. But pretending to be sick is useless. The camera on the ceiling above the door reminds me of that.

I shrug and pretend that angering a murderer is not a big deal. "It's fine. I can handle it."

He looks as though he's about to leave me to it, but a tube slips from his grasp and tumbles to the tiled floor. I swoop down and pick it up for him just as he attempts to retrieve it himself, and our fingers brush. And then linger. One second, two seconds. A grin, wild like his hair, spreads across his face. For a moment, I live in that grin and the joy that it brings to my pounding heart.

"I, I uh, I haven't seen you in the cafeteria lately," he says. "Kind of miss eating with you."

I blush. We only ate together once, and that was the time I was under the effects of whatever drug goes into the food. I straighten and allow him to take the tube.

"Was hoping I'd get a chance to ask you something."

"Ask me something?" I get my hopes up. "What about?"

"Well, I was wondering…" He half-smiles and runs a hand slowly through his cropped curls, almost dropping two tubes this time. "There's a band playing this Friday, down at the SPC. I mean, the Sparkstone Performance

Centre. SPC. Anyway, we don't get too many bands willing to come this far north, but uh, I was able to get an extra ticket before they sold out." Holding the mess of tubes tightly to his chest, he reaches his free hand into his pocket and pulls out two tickets printed on light blue paper. "Not sure really if they're going to be any good or anything, but I didn't really want to go alone, so if you were available—"

"Yes. I can be available."

"Oh! Great." He looks relieved. "I'll just hold onto these then. This is…this is really good." Then, much quieter: "I was hoping you'd say yes."

I purse my lips to stop myself from singing with joy. I'm about to say something witty in reply when someone calls Ethan's name. He turns, and I peer around him. A girl, maybe a year or two older than I am, comes down the stairs at the end of the hall. Her shoulder-length black hair bounces as she runs. A single strand is braided down her left side, as if she's a Jedi Padawan. Too artsy to be a Jedi, though. Her skinny jeans have colourful patches on the knees, and her paint-stained white shirt falls off one shoulder.

Ethan's face lights up as he awkwardly waves back and stuffs the tickets back into his pocket. She grins, and as she approaches Ethan, her arm slips briefly through his, careful not to disturb the tubes. He nudges her playfully and she retracts her grasp. They're both smiling.

A pang of jealousy stabs my already queasy stomach.

"You're going to be late," she says to him. Her accent sounds American and her words fire quick from her lips. "Walk me there?"

He exaggerates an eye roll. "You just want help carrying

your canvases. You see how many I got now? Typical. I can't carry anything else."

She eyes his tubes. "I can't help it if I'm a more prolific painter than you."

Ethan seems to remember that I'm standing in front of him. "Oh, Ingrid, you haven't met Kimberly yet, have you?"

I shake my head, vaguely recalling her name mentioned a few days ago. Might as well have been a few years ago, with all that I've been through.

She holds out a polite hand. She's wearing a ring on her middle finger that holds a blue gem the size of my eyeball. I shake her hand and wonder if the gem is real.

"Ethan told me about you," she says as a sly smile slides across her flawless dark skin.

Oh great. So she knows how I threw myself at Ethan and made out with him in the middle of the field in the wee hours of the morning just because I thought I was dead and going to Heaven.

"Nice to meet you," I manage to say through my embarrassment. "So, um, you and Ethan are in the same...tutorial? You have the same major?"

"Not the same tutorial, no, but we have a similar major, yes. Have you seen his paintings? They are *gorgeous*. You should come by the studio sometime. I'll show you mine."

She talks a mile a minute, gesturing excitedly, and the beads around her neck click and clack and tangle as she moves. Smiling, she shakes Ethan's arm and almost upsets his delicate grasp on his tubes. "Are you almost done the one you started a couple days ago? You *have* to show her that one. It's absolutely beautiful. Is it in one of these tubes?"

"Um, no, not quite done yet. Maybe when it's finished

you can come see it." Now it's his turn to look a little uncomfortable. He readjusts his grip.

"Sure. As long as I'm not intruding in your space or anything."

"No, no, of course not! You can come any time. Any time I'm not racing to finish an assignment or anything. Unless that's a good time for you. I guess I could—" Ethan stops babbling suddenly. His eyes widen. "Oh *shoot!* I was supposed to have a meeting with Ms. Agailya this morning." Ethan checks his watch. "Bloody hell, a half hour ago. And my tutorial is starting. Sorry Ingrid, I have to go."

I mumble a goodbye but he's not really paying attention to me anymore.

"You're *always* forgetting!" Kimberly exclaims, throwing her hands up in the air in exasperation. "Just write it down. You're like, the most disorganized, head-in-the-clouds guy on the planet. Here, at least let me help you with those tubes before you embarrass yourself."

Her ribbing continues and fades as they disappear down the hallway. I shouldn't be jealous. I bet Ethan's not jealous that one of my new friends is a guy. And Ethan did just ask me on a date, basically. He is interested in me.

Right?

God, I hope he's not one of those guys who just hangs out with girls for the attention.

My attention shifts to Room 216. I am *so* late for tutorial.

I push the door open and interrupt Jia midsentence. She's talking about her meta-analysis paper on child psychology research, which she's writing in addition to this semester's project. She only falters for a moment, but the door opening trumpets my arrival on its own. Jadore rises from her chair, positioned in front of the semicircle of students, and slowly pivots to face me. Jia's words peter out as Jadore fixes her gaze upon me.

"Late, very late," Jadore says.

CHAPTER 2

Even though her soulless, dark eyes are hidden behind thick shades, fear clutches my heart when she turns her head my way. She rises slowly, with one hand steady on her cane. Her look stops me dead in the doorway, and my insides freeze. To the rest of the students here at Sparkstone, Professor Jadore is blind. I know better. Her black eyes, filled with anger and death, can't be obscured by whatever technology she's using to cloak the rest of her body.

She's tall, and the more I stare at her, the more similarities I see between her human and alien forms. Her copper skin is oily and almost shimmers in the light shining through the window, as though it's struggling to stay attached to her muscle and bone.

"Take a seat, Ingrid. The world does not wait for you."

No one questions how she knows it's me. I gulp and sit in an empty chair at one end of the semicircle. Misty, Jia, and Wil are on the other side, and they do a good job of ignoring me. The less they seem to care about me, the less leverage Jadore and the Collective have over me. In theory.

"I was considering letting you all out early today," Jadore says, tapping her long nails against her cane. "But given someone's lack of regard for our time, we will stay."

All the girls in the tutorial except Jia and Misty throw me annoyed looks. My face burns. I'm not supposed to be the ostracized girl. I'm supposed to be the smart one who doesn't ask questions and gets A-plus on everything. I hate this image that Jadore is painting of me. I want out.

Jadore begins a discussion about another girl's project, a chemistry paper. Part of me wants to take diligent notes as the rest of the students critique her description and approach to the problem. The other part of me wants to scheme ways to expose Jadore's lack of blindness to the tutorial so that for once, I am the hero and not the villain in this group.

I fix my gaze on my notebook. *"Avoid unnecessary jargon"* is the last entry. My pen carefully and delicately traces the letters so that it looks as if I'm doing something useful.

"Ingrid." Jadore lances me in the stomach with my own name. "Give us an update on where you are with your project. You must be making steady progress if you insist on being tardy."

My project has been going nowhere fast. In a desperate attempt to show Jadore that I was not afraid of her, I told her last week in front of the whole tutorial that I was going to do a project on Joseph G. Campbell—a mysterious man who is probably an alien—and his theory on multiverses and the effect of travel between potential multiple universes on the human brain. Do I know what the multiverse theory is? Science fiction, that's what it is, but it pulls deep strings within me, strings that are attached to my favourite TV shows, such as *Doctor Who* and *Battlestar Galactica*. Unfortunately, science fiction is not science fact. I have no information to report on Joseph G. Campbell except what is in Sunni's journal, which I'm not supposed to have. But I have been doing some research on the human brain, and how it works.

"Um... sure." I clear my throat to buy me three seconds. It's not really enough. I flip a few pages in my notebook and find my project notes. "The human brain accounts for about twenty percent of the body's energy usage. Recent studies have shown that, uh, neurons in the brain actually use a bunch of energy to send signals. So, I theorize that if we assume that the multiverse theory is correct, and one can travel between universes"—I gulp, knowing how silly I sound—"and not knowing how long the actual travelling takes, we can surmise that we would probably need more energy than actually calculated, because the body will probably use it up just to stay alive during transit."

I'm out of my depth, and Jadore knows it. The other students seem either embarrassed or bored. One girl is even playing on her cell phone. I guess she thinks she can get away with that.

You should've stayed away from mentioning energy and calculations. No doubt any scientist would take body energy into consideration when calculating what is needed to transport someone from one place to another, Wil says to me telepathically, as he pretends to look disinterested. *You should also always have calculations ready to show her. I can help you with that, if you need it. Unfortunately it's too late for you today.*

Jadore is silent. Too silent. But I don't look away from her sunglasses. I don't want her to think that I'm not trying, that I am stupid. I feel numb. We haven't really spoken since she admitted she knew we'd visited the mother ship last week. Some of the girls in the circle throw me covert pity glances. I wrap their looks around the goosebumps on my arms.

"Ingrid, you will stay with me after tutorial so we can further discuss your...theories." The word *theories* bites my ears. She raps her cane against the side of her chair. "Next."

The tutorial is a mess of voices and information weaving between the folds of my brain but not sticking around long enough to be processed. I doodle in my notebook, beside the bullet point notes I'd made about the human brain. It's not going to be enough to impress Jadore. She will demand more of me. She will probably threaten me with my friends' lives again. Or something much worse.

Breathe in, breathe out. *Only five more minutes, and then another ten with Jadore, and then you are as free as you are ever going to be.*

Those five minutes are five seconds to my internal clock. Before I know it, Jadore is dismissing the other students. Jia, Wil, and Misty are careful not to show any signs that they care about me as they leave the classroom, even though I need their friendship more than ever as I stare Sunni's murderer in the face.

"So," Jadore says, thumping her cane once on the floor. "What progress have you made on your project? Other than that textbook dribble you recited to me."

I curl my lips. "No progress."

Jadore considers this. "Hmmph," she says. *Thunk* goes her cane. She paces before the semicircle of chairs that once held my peers. "Your profile did not say you were *lazy*."

"I'm not lazy."

She smiles, and I feel dumb. I'd fallen for her attempt to make me angry. I have to be more careful with what I say. I have to be like her, in control of what my face looks like to others.

I take a deep breath. I have to play along, just a little bit, if I'm going to find out anything about Joseph G. Campbell. "I lack direction, that's all."

"Really," Jadore says. She sounds unconvinced. "And what would you like for me to do about that?"

I stand. With my boots on, bring my height to just below her nose. I ball my fingers into fists because it makes me feel more confident. "You are my supervisor for this project. You are supposed to do your job."

Jadore lets out a bitter laugh. "You think you can use me? You are sorely mistaken." Her lips part slowly, and out comes her thin, forked tongue. It tastes the air. "You know more about him than you let on, Ingrid. I can smell the knowledge inside you. He has *touched* you somehow. I can taste his scent."

Touched me? My stomach is a jumbled mess of fear, but the words scroll across my mind: *She's telling the truth. Somehow, deep down, you know him. You've always known him. His face is burned into your memory. He haunts your dreams but he will not rescue you from your nightmares.*

"Find Campbell," Jadore says. "Find him, and I'll give you an A *plus*."

I snort. "Why should I care about grades here?"

"You do want a job when you leave, don't you?"

"You mean *leaving* is an option?"

Jadore smirks. "Ingrid. Don't make me send you home to live with your parents."

"I love my parents." *And I sure would like to go home.*

"You can live there, for the rest of your days, while your friends go on and excel in their chosen fields."

She's being sarcastic—I think. The students exhibiting signs of an active Gene 213 are harvested. I have a hard time imagining many graduates—if there are many at all—enjoying their chosen fields for very long.

"I could find my own way."

"Could you?" Jadore raises two neatly plucked eyebrows. "You're certain that other universities would accept you? That other prestigious places of employment would have you?"

"Why wouldn't they?"

"All your other universities of choice rejected you. Do you think that's a coincidence?"

My stomach swims with dread. I should have known. The Collective's influence stretches around the world. All Jadore has to do is whisper in the right ears, and my future will be flushed down the drain. Not even flushed—more like deposited into her greedy, scaly hands.

Jadore regards my silence with a smug smile. "I see we've come to an understanding. You do as I say, when I say, and you will be treated well, for as long as you are useful."

Her words sound far away. They're staining my life, tainting it. *I'll be treated well, for as long as I'm useful.* She's assigning value to my life. Making it worthless. I am hers to do with as she pleases, until she dissects me for my precious genes.

But my life is not worthless. I have so much to live for. I can't let her get to me, not like this.

I whip around and head for the door.

"Where are you going, Ingrid? I haven't dismissed you yet."

I grit my teeth. "I have *research* to do."

"I did not say you could leave."

I look over my shoulder at her and drive daggers into her face with my stare. Jadore takes a careful step towards me.

"You are *mine*," she says. "Remember that."

I'm seething, but anything I say could make my current situation worse. "I know," I say with as much insolence as I can muster through my fear.

"I am glad we have that established," she replies. There's venom in her tone.

My eyes narrow, and I turn to leave again.

"Ah ah!" Jadore says. I blink, and she's before me, her copper hand splayed across the doorknob. "What did I just say about being dismissed?"

That's it. I'm getting tired of these games. She might be in control of my future, and she might have the power to kill me with the snap of a finger, but I refuse to be treated like a pet that barks on command. I grab her hand and throw it away from the knob.

Raging, Jadore digs her long black fingernails into my neck and slams me against the wall next to the door. I see my frightened, surprised face reflected in her sunglasses. She's stronger than she looks. I gasp for air as she holds me against the wall with one hand and raises her cane with the other. A *click*, and then a *shing* as a small blade no longer than my middle finger rises from the tip of the cane. It glints in the light.

Her face is centimetres from mine. She smells like wet

earth and something else, something chemical, sort of like spoiled cream, but with a metal undercurrent. The smell fires off a series of colours in my synesthetic brain: browns, dark reds, and bubbly dark greens, all full of poison.

"Try to escape. Try it. I *dare* you," she hisses in my ear. "You won't even make it past the gate." She chuckles. The sound is uncomfortably warm. "If you make it past the gate, forget about the project. You'll get your A-plus and I'll even let your friends go free."

I struggle to breathe. She tightens her grip. I writhe and kick, aiming for her stomach. She leaps back to avoid my blow and then releases me. I turn, throw open the door, and run.

Escape, and I can go free. There are almost no students in the hallway, and I zoom down the corridor, round a corner, and out of the building. If I can make it to the gate...

She's still playing me. This is just a game to her. She'll never let my friends go free. She'll never let me go free.

I run faster. Cramps are already attacking my sides. But maybe, just maybe, I *can* get out of here. Jadore's not going to give me the information I need, I know this now. She's going to use me like a paper towel, make me do all of her dirty work and then dispose of me when I'm no longer useful. I can always find out more about Joseph G. Campbell when I escape.

What about Sunni's journal?

Shoot. There's no time to go back for that. I pass the greenhouse that Misty almost destroyed with her fire a few days ago and see that it looks brand new. Sparkstone University leaves no evidence of any strange occurrences behind. I cross the road and there's a loud *HONK*. A car narrowly misses me. I wave an apology but there's no time. I'm maybe five—maybe ten—minutes away from freedom.

My boots clunk on the sidewalk, and my feet protest in the high heels, but I push them faster. My lungs are burning. The gate, I can *see* it. I can *see* my freedom.

And then my cell phone vibrates.

Maybe it's Ethan, I think as I draw the phone from my pocket. *And now I'll have to mumble another awkward goodbye. Maybe Jadore will release him too, if I can get free…*

But the number on my screen isn't Ethan's. It's my mum's cell phone number.

My stomach ties itself into knots as I answer the phone. "Mum? Hello?"

"Ingrid!" She sounds worried. Distressed. "Listen to me. Something—"

"Mum, I really…really need you to come…get me." I'm a bit out of breath. The gate is *so* close. Another street, maybe two, and then—

"What? No. Ingrid, your father is in the hospital!"

I stop so suddenly that I almost trip. My vision fills with black and white dots. I'm about to faint. "Hospital…"

"Yes. It all happened so quickly! He just dropped me off at the mall, and then he pulled out onto MacLeod Trail and out of nowhere this large truck comes and slams into him. The car in front of him was braking for a light and so your father rear-ended him, and…it was so fast, Ingrid. I don't know…I don't know…" Her voice cracks. She's on the edge of tears.

I put one foot in front of the other. Anything to keep

moving. Maybe I can still make it to the gate. My fast-walking turns into a run. *My dad is in the hospital.*

"Is he going to be okay?"

"I don't know, Ingrid. I'm just getting into the ambulance right now. He's... he's unconscious. The paramedics just keep telling me to be calm, and they're injecting your father with some kind of pain medication. It looks green and awful and I keep asking them what it is and they tell me it's for the pain but I've never, ever seen anything like this before—"

"What? That doesn't sound—"

My heart nearly stops. I can see the entrance to the gate. I can even see Ohz, in his creepy human form. He's standing on the other side, gripping the bars, smiling a toothy grin at me.

I hear Mum talking to the paramedics, trying to get more information, and the sirens and sounds of shuffling and movement as they try to save my father. But I know the truth. The Collective is everywhere. Somehow, in mere minutes, they made this happen. They have my father in their clutches now. And they're not going to let him go.

I walk right up to the gate. I am here. Ohz makes some sort of gurgling sound, like laughter. A drop of saliva falls from his opened mouth. He knows I am trapped, and he is enjoying watching me suffer.

"Mum, you have to come get me," I say as calmly as I can manage. A tear escapes my left eye.

"That's out of the question. I'm in an ambulance, with your father. The car is totalled. I won't leave him." Her voice breaks. "I'm... I'm sorry, Ingrid. I'll come as soon as I can. Maybe when your father wakes up. You can see him then. But I can't just *leave.*"

Of course she can't.

I can't leave either.

The message is clear. *You walk through that gate, we kill your father.*

Beyond the gate, open plains. No proper civilization for kilometres. Jadore was right. I can run all I want. But I'm not going anywhere.

I sob silently so Mum can't hear, grip a bar of the golden gate—the gilded cage that holds me captive—and press my forehead hard against the metal. It's cold, despite the warm air. The gate shakes with my sobs.

"Ingrid? Are you still there?" My mother's voice is small in my ear.

"Mhmmm," I say, wiping my nose. I turn away from Ohz because I hate him seeing me weak.

"We're almost to the hospital. I'll call you when he's settled. Okay? Then we can talk about you coming home. Does Sparkstone have a shuttle service? They should, they're so far out. Maybe one of the professors can drive you to Edmonton and you can get a flight from there, or maybe I could somehow rent you a car—"

There are people behind me. Three maintenance workers, wearing the same blue overalls as Ohz. Greedy hunger is written all over their faces. One of them is holding what looks like a taser. Another silent threat.

I take a deep breath and say the hardest words I've ever had to say. "No, Mum. Don't . . . don't worry about me. I'm fine."

"Are you sure, honey? You said you wanted me to come get you. Is something wrong? Has something happened to you too? Oh God, I don't think I could take it if—"

The maintenance worker with the taser raises the weapon slowly.

"No, Mum. I just…I was just thinking about you, that's all." Another sob wells in my throat. My cheeks are soaked with tears. "I just miss you. And Dad. And home. Someday I'll come home. I promise."

"Of course, honey. And maybe when your father is better—he *will* get better, there's so much blood but it can't be as bad as it looks, it just can't be!—we'll come for a visit, okay?"

I shake my head. *My parents will never set foot on Sparkstone soil.* But she can't hear my thoughts.

I look the maintenance worker with the taser square in the eye. My vision blurs with the tears but I swallow my fear. "I will go home someday," I say, both to my mother and the alien before me. "Not today." I choke on a sob. "But I swear, I'll go home, one day."

"I know, honey, I know."

She's crying again, and I let myself cry too. The alien maintenance workers stare at me, still as mannequins.

"End the call," says Ohz behind me. "Crosskey must return to Mistress."

"I have to go now, Mum," I say. My hands are shaking and my palms are sweaty. "I'll talk to you later."

"I'll call you," she says. "The ambulance is just pulling up now—"

"Okay, Mum. I love you." I grit my teeth and press the phone hard against my ear, afraid that the aliens will take away my mother's voice as well as my father's life.

"Love you too, Ingrid."

And just as one of them reaches for the phone, I press the end call button and shove the phone down my shirt, into my bra. I cross my arms fiercely against my chest. They won't take my cell phone away. They can't. I won't let them.

Fortunately, the alien retracts his hand. "You will come with us, now."

They flank me and I have no choice. I'm led through the town, all the way back to Sparkstone campus. I can't bear to look up and see who could be watching, and what they might be thinking. First, I'm humiliated in tutorial. Now, I'm paraded through the town, as if I'm some kind of troublemaker.

Jadore is waiting for me in front of Rogers Hall. Some of the maintenance workers disband and go back to their duties, but two remain—one on either side of me. She saunters towards me with her cane's help, pushing her shoulders back to ensure that she towers over me even more than usual. I refuse to grace her with my gaze.

"T*sssssk tssssssk*, Ingrid," Jadore says, and flicks her forked tongue hungrily. Her *s*'s are elongated. "I heard what happened to your father. A shame you can't be there."

I'm shaking with rage. "You did something to him."

She feigns innocence. "*You* are the one who ran."

"And you—"

"Find Campbell. Or else..." She squeezes her hand into a fist, and I get the message: *Or else I'll make sure your father never leaves that hospital alive.*

CHAPTER 3

I repeat Wil's name over and over in my mind. I don't know if he can hear me. I don't really care. But I need someone right now. And it can't be Ethan. I would never let him see me like this. My new friends are the only ones who could possibly know how I feel.

When I reach my room, they're already at the door, waiting. Wil heard me after all. I swipe my key card and can barely contain myself. There's a camera in the corner just above the door, but the red light has been silenced—no doubt by Wil's mind.

I beeline for the bed and sink into the comforter. Jia, Misty, and Wil file in, and Wil shuts the door carefully behind him. His dark eyes scan the room quickly to neutralize any other alien cameras or devices that might be privy to our conversation. Jia takes a seat to my left on the bed. With only a look, she implores me to speak. My mouth is dry, unlike my cheeks.

"They have my dad," I whisper.

Jia grabs my left hand and squeezes it. Wil sits on my right and pulls me into hug. I bury my face in his muscular shoulder. He brushes a strand of hair behind my ear, and his fingers linger at my temple.

"I can try to make the pain go away," he says. "If you want it."

"You can?" Of course he can. He can interface with my brain and tell my body to stop panicking, to stop feeling. It would be easier that way.

"No," I say finally, sitting up, drawing away from him. "I need something to remind me of why I'm here."

"Mmm." Misty grunts from across the room. She pushes herself off the wall adjacent to the door and takes a few hesitant but strong steps towards me. Her arms are folded, her hands balled into fists. No reassurance from her. But she wears Sunni's death on her sleeve as a reminder of Sparkstone's cruelty and injustice.

With some prompting from Jia, I quickly tell them what happened between me and Jadore—how she manipulated me into running, how she let me know I am a glorified slave. "I feel so stupid," I say at the end of my story, tugging at my long locks of red hair.

"Don't," Wil says. "That's how she wants you to feel."

"If she gets to you, then she has already won," Jia says in a voice that sounds years older than her actual age.

"Maybe," I say. "They won't hesitate to kill him if I'm caught doing something rash. They could make his death look natural, or accidental. They do have access to technology we barely understand." I fiddle with the silver band around my wrist. We all wear matching ones. It helped me sneak onto the mother ship days ago, and I haven't been able to get it off since. Fortunately it seems to be waterproof and looks like a silver bangle if not examined too closely. "I should've activated the alien band when I started running. Then maybe I would've had a chance."

Jia opens her mouth to offer more reassurance when Misty pipes up. "At least you made it to the gate."

I lift my gaze, and Misty is biting her nails again. She raises her thinly plucked eyebrows, as if giving me permission to initiate a line of questioning.

"You tried to *escape*?" I ask.

Misty cracks a nasty smile. "Yeah, I tried." She lifts her shirt, and there's a large circular red scar above her stomach. "Taser. Probably the only scar I'm proud of."

"You have other..." I stop myself. I know better than to ask about Misty's past. With her temper, I wouldn't be surprised about what sort of trouble she's gotten herself into. "They *tased* you?" And I thought I had it hard. They just pointed the taser at me.

"Yeah. I guess some of the security guards are authorized to carry tasers for some of the "unruly" students."

"It shouldn't be allowed! How can the students stand by and let this happen? Isn't there a student council, or a student union?"

"Of course there isn't. This is Sparkstone we're talkin' about here, remember?"

Jia smiles wanly. "The food keeps them complacent, we think. Regardless, most are too happy to study what they wish and be surrounded by intelligent minds with the promise of a bright future to be bothered with the problems of others."

I stand and walk to the window that overlooks Rogers Hall. The day has become overcast and gloomy, and rainclouds hover in the distance over the great expanse of the prairies.

"Then maybe we should *make* a student council," I say quietly.

"Good luck with that," Wil says.

"You're not going to help me?" My hand clenches the edge of the windowsill. "Jadore thinks we're livestock. Our only advantage is that they need us alive, at least until we show signs of superhuman abilities. If we were able to organize the students, create some kind of, well, a movement...or a protest..."

"Jadore will shut you down in a heartbeat," he replies.

Jia looks thoughtful. "Not if we get another professor on our side."

I don't have Wil's power over thoughts, but I know exactly whom Jia is thinking about. "Ms. Agailya."

"She won't help us," Misty mutters.

"But she might."

"She won't," Misty says, more certain this time. "She had her chance, before. She didn't help us back then, she won't help us now."

"Why, what happened before?"

Wil's stare falls to the floor, and Misty continues picking at her nail polish.

"I'll help you, Ingrid," Jia says. "Jadore may have threatened the well-being of our families and the well-being of the students here, but we have to be willing to push back. We aren't the only ones who want more of a say at the school. There must be others like us."

Wil stands wearily while running a hand over his smoothly shaved head. "I feel like I would've sensed other Sparks like us. But I am working on something else that could help us. Jia, could you book the library study room for tomorrow, and we can talk about this then?"

Her finger taps her cheek as she nods. I glance up at the camera. It's blinking red again. No more candid conversations.

Wil heads for the door. "If you need anything else...just call."

"Sure." I bunch my blankets in a fist as he leaves, followed by Misty. Jia lingers.

"Rain check on that run?" she asks.

I smile gratefully. "Yeah. Thanks."

She nods and closes the door after her. When their footsteps have retreated down the hallway, I flop on the bed and bury my face in the blankets. I wish life were like a computer game, and then I could reload a save from a year ago. A year would be enough for me to screw up all of my grade twelve marks so I could avoid the Collective's gaze. If I could rewrite history like that, I'd probably be settling into some other *real* prestigious university, one not controlled by aliens.

I roll over. And where would that have left everyone? If I hadn't come to Sparkstone, the Collective wouldn't have been able to use my brain to transmit a musical signal, a ruse that led the Sparks into a trap. I'd be blissfully unaware of the intelligent—albeit, mostly malevolent—life above us at this very moment. But the Collective might still have captured Sunni, and she still might have died.

Sunni knew I'd come, as she saw it in a vision. Would Fate find a way to subvert my plans, no matter what? I launch myself from the bed. It's pointless to think about, really. My dad is fighting for his life, and I'm stuck here hundreds of miles away. I need to make the best of this, if there is a best of it.

The camera's red light is prominent today. I glare at it defiantly. There is one thing I can try to do, even with them watching.

I close my eyes and concentrate on teleporting across my dorm room.

It's a hopeless exercise. Stupid, really. Just because I did it that one time, a few days ago, on a doomed ship floating in space, doesn't mean I can do it again, here on Earth.

At least, I'm pretty sure I teleported. One moment I was staring at the Earth, late evening northern Alberta time, and the next thing I knew, the sun was rising and I was waking up just outside of Sparkstone campus. What happened in those seven or eight hours, I don't know. I dread the idea that it could take that long for me to teleport from point A to point B. Maybe I teleported and then fell asleep when I landed.

I squeeze my eyes shut and try again. My dorm room is approximately fifteen steps wide. I have paced it often in the last few days. I want to transport myself two steps from the wall.

Concentrate. Relax. I want to be two steps from the wall of my dorm room in Sparkstone, Alberta.

I exhale my frustrations, but it doesn't help. No matter how much I will myself, I'm not getting any closer to the other side of my room. For all I know, this power I supposedly have is random. I might wake up a few hours from now with Ethan's gorgeous face hovering over mine as I lie helpless in the middle of a field.

Ethan...

Thinking about him last time brought me back to Earth. Brought me back to *him*. What if I tried that again?

"What are you doing?"

My eyes fly open, and Misty is standing in the doorway. She's biting her nails and challenging me with her dark blue eyes. The long-sleeved black shirt she's wearing is set askew and bares one of her shoulders. There's a thin red scar there, probably from a battle she's fought, with the Sparks or otherwise. That makes two scars I've seen on her today.

"I'm…I'm just…" I hide my hands behind my back as if I'm holding something incriminating. "Nothing."

"Uh-huh." Misty doesn't even bother to question me further. "Well, I just forgot my sweater."

She crosses the room to retrieve a black hoodie propped against the windowsill. I hadn't even noticed she was wearing one, I was so distraught. As she slides an arm into the sleeve, her bare wrist peeks from beneath the protection of her sleeve and reveals another story I can't bring myself to ask her about. A faded pink scar blazes across the prominent blue vein and is surrounded by tinier whiter scars. It's like a small galaxy of shooting stars that have lost their sense of direction and now streak aimlessly across the universe.

I look away before she can harass me for wondering about things that aren't my business. The scars look years old at least. I wonder what she must have gone through to be that desperate to end this life, especially since she has an incredible gift.

"Jia and Wil and I are going to order some lunch," she says unenthusiastically, as though it's a chore to tell me this. "Don't suppose you're in any shape to join us?"

I hug my chest and think about my dwindling cash. It seems like we only ate breakfast two hours ago. Not that a croissant is much of a breakfast. "Um, I don't really know..."

She zips up the hoodie. I'm surprised she hasn't left yet. Misty and I have barely had a real conversation since Sunni's death. She eyes my half-unpacked suitcase beside the window. "You seem to be making yourself at home."

Guilt balls up in my stomach. The Collective took everything of Sunni's in this room, and I have done nothing to restore our friend's presence. Misty probably thinks I've forgotten about Sunni. "Well... I'm not going to live out of my suitcase for the rest of the year."

"Rest of the *four* years," Misty reminds me with a stiff growl. "There ain't no apartments in Sparkstone. Just expensive housing that ain't available for even the wealthiest students." She says that word, *wealthiest*, with malice, and sweeps her gaze over my instruments—the keyboard next to the dresser and the harp next to the suitcase.

I try to ignore the silent insult. It's not that my parents are super rich or anything. Sure, they could afford to send me to lessons at the Royal Conservatory for both piano and harp. My cheeks heat. I guess I did have it pretty good. Then again, I can only judge Misty by what little I know of her, which, besides the whole alien invasion/teens-with-superpowers thing, is very little. I have no idea if Misty is actually jealous of my apparent wealth or if she's just being her bitter, sarcastic self.

Her family must have money if she's here, I think as I grab a random shirt from my suitcase to busy my hands. *The tuition is not cheap, as Dad likes to remind me. Unless Sparkstone has generous scholarship programs, to lure its guinea pigs here.*

Thinking about my father reopens the wound. I squeeze my eyes shut to push it from my mind but open them again as Misty scuffs her muddy boots across the carpet. "So. You comin' or what?"

I lift my eyebrows. "Coming? I mean…going? Where?"

She glares at me. "Words just going in through one ear and out the other today for ya? It's lunch time. You coming to lunch, or am I just wasting my time here?"

I place the shirt in a half-empty dresser drawer and shut it. The dresser wobbles. Next to the dresser is the bathroom, where Sunni's journal is hiding in a sealed plastic bag in the toilet tank. I hate leaving the room without it, but carrying it around would be too suspicious, and I can't stay cooped up in here all the time. I have a part to play. New friends to protect. I nod at Misty. "Let me get my purse."

She grunts something unintelligible, maybe in another language. I fetch my purse from under the bed and then remember that I've left my backpack and my notebook in the tutorial classroom. Stupid, stupid me. I'll have to get it later. At least my laptop is still here.

Misty waits impatiently, tapping her muddy boot on the carpet some more.

"You know, there's a doormat outside. You could've wiped your feet."

Her eyes flick down to the mess she's created on the carpet. Another scowl. She knows I'm right. I hang my purse on my shoulder as Misty storms out of the room. I sigh. The mud isn't really a big deal. But I have a feeling that she would've been more considerate if this room were still Sunni's.

She probably feels like I'm replacing her. I guess I sort of am, in a way. The thought stings. I tug on my knee-high boots. We're all struggling with Sunni's death, but Misty's taking it especially hard. I should try to be nicer to her.

After ensuring my dorm room is locked with my electronic key card, I join Misty in the hallway. I'm surprised she's still waiting. Leaning up against the wall, arms folded, she looks as if she's waiting for trouble to happen. Her fingers dance over her hoodie. She's recently ripped the nail off her left forefinger. It's bleeding.

"Ready?" she asks.

"Yes. Thanks for waiting for me. You didn't have to."

"Whatever."

I sigh and start down the hallway. "I didn't mean it like that. You didn't have to come get me for lunch, but you did. And you didn't have to wait, but you did. And you didn't have to come and try to comfort me, but you did that too. So...thanks."

She shrugs.

This being-nice-to-Misty business is going to be harder than I thought.

～෧

Lunch is quick, and I buy the cheapest thing on the menu. Jia tries to get me to eat more, but I'm too distraught to think about my stomach. I excuse myself early and walk back to Rita House.

I'm glad that I don't have tutorial tomorrow. Fortunately I only have to put up with Jadore four times a week. Tuesdays, as well as weekends, I'm free from her tyranny. It's just Sparkstone's tyranny in general I have to deal with. I try not to look at the camera as I cross the lobby and head towards the stairs.

"Ingrid Stanley?"

The soft voice carries through the echoing lobby and freezes my heart. My legs stop moving. Ms. Agailya slides into view out of an office behind the main security desk, looking as ethereal as ever. Today her long silver-blonde hair is braided over one shoulder. She hides her thin figure beneath a white knitted cardigan and a billowing vibrant-blue skirt. In her left hand, she carries a clipboard filled with neatly arranged papers.

I clear my throat. "Did you need me for something?"

Her eyes are warm and inviting. "You have been with us for a week. I merely wanted to know how you were adjusting."

Her accent is Spanish or French, though she's definitely not European. We're fairly certain that like Jadore, Ms. Agailya is an alien incognito. Whatever her real race is, I'm convinced they must be a peaceful people, because being in Ms. Agailya's presence is like sitting on a sunny beach and listening to the waves crash up against the shore. Regardless of how her presence feels, there's a little voice in my head telling me not to trust any of the professors. Who knows what their real agenda is.

"It's been pretty good," I say, mustering a smile. The shorter I keep this conversation, the better. There's a camera almost directly to our left, and everything we say is on the record.

"You are comfortable, then?"

About as comfortable as you can be after you witness a girl being murdered by one of the professors, in space.

I draw a deep breath so that I can sound convincing. "I'm fine."

Ms. Agailya's smile is thin. "Your new room is to your satisfaction?"

Sunni's old room. I'm just replacing her, another collection of organs and tissue to be harvested when the time is right. I nod slowly, because if I speak, my voice will break and I think I'll scream.

"Professor Jadore has told me of your project." Ms. Agailya's gaze runs down a page on her clipboard. "I have some free time tomorrow afternoon to discuss your major with you. If you already know your second major, we can discuss this as well. Is this acceptable, Ingrid?"

Second major. Right. I haven't even thought about what I want to declare. Does my decision even matter at all?

"Yeah. Fine."

"I will see you then," she says in her silvery voice, and glides away, back into her office.

Thinking about my major is the last thing I want to do right now. But research of any kind will take my mind off my father and may please Jadore enough to make her spare his life—if she's feeling generous. I grit my teeth and steel my spirit as I run all the way back to my dorm room and prepare myself for a long afternoon and evening of research.

I blink, and with a ripple, Sparkstone's mysterious underground library creates itself before my eyes, like dominos falling upward and upright, playing on rewind. The aisle I'm treading through has shelves almost to the ceiling this time, packed solidly with books that have gibberish printed on their spines. The date is still etched into the shelves as well, warning me that Saturday, September thirteenth is the date of the library's demise. Less than a week away in the real world.

I don't have to glance over my shoulder, because I feel Sunni's presence already.

We're back again, I say to her.

"We're still here," she replies. "We've never left, and we will always be here, even when we are gone."

In the real world, I would've questioned her logic further, but here, I accept it as gospel. *Are we going to see Campbell's eye again?*

"Well, that's up to you, isn't it?"

I don't think so.

On the floor, vines creep and slither around the bases of the bookshelves. Curious, I follow them and find the clearing that was made before, when I was here last. The largest maple tree I've ever seen has usurped Campbell's eye. Its roots—the vines, I realize—stretch into the aisles of shelves, while only a privileged few dig into the tiled floor. The stark red leaves contrast the green light from the glass ceiling and canopy the clearing as if the maple tree's ancestor were a willow tree.

The trunk is at least three times wider than I can spread my arms, and I circle part of the way around until I find what I know is there—the outline of a door, etched into the tree bark. A door, leading inside the tree. It glows in greeting when I find it, like some sort of large, sideways, perverted, angled smile. It's always waiting for me. It will always wait for me.

"Open it," Sunni insists, as she always does.

Why? What will happen if I do? What happens if I don't go through the door?

"You already have," says a deep voice that isn't Sunni's.

It's a voice I know instinctively to be Campbell's, even though it is oddly distorted and sounds like a mix of my father's voice, and Ethan's voice, and Wil's voice. He is drawing on voices that I know to create a new voice, because he doesn't have one, not yet. It's coming from the other side of the door, from the heart of the tree.

"Everything that will happen," Campbell continues in his borrowed voice, "has already happened, and will happen again. I just have to get there first."

What does that mean?

From the crack in the door, a flurry of pages flies out and circles me like a swarm of insects. The swarm is short-lived, however, as the pages assemble themselves neatly and bind into a book with an old brown-blue leather cover. It looks similar to Sunni's journal, but I can tell that it is older than anything I can imagine, that this book has been through wars, and has weathered much just to be lying in my grasp right now. I can feel it physically in my hands in the real world as well.

Sunni looks interested, and draws nearer to me. "I was looking for that. And now you found it!"

I flip through the pages. They are just as weathered as the cover. Handwritten in elegant script, in large letters on every page, is *"HOW TO SAVE HER."*

How to save who? Sunni? Me? Misty? Jia? Is it a question, or a declaration?

"You need this book. This book…it is part of his soul," Sunni explains quickly. Her twang is so clear, clearer than it's ever been here. "It has the answer to what the Collective wants at Sparkstone."

I can't take this back with me, can I, I say, knowing the answer.

"Everything you need to find it, you already have," she replies. She grips me tighter. "And one more thing."

I shake my head and pull away from her. *Don't tell me...*

"I have to. You have to *go through the door.*"

No, why Sunni, why—?

"It's the only way..."

She begins to morph into Jadore. I fall to the floor and curl into a ball, protecting Campbell's book with my body. *It's time for me to leave now. Please, spare me this part. Please...*

˚

My wish is granted. I gasp and grip my sheets as I sit up in bed. That book, Campbell's book, I felt it. It was real. I had it in my grasp.

A cold breeze whips through the room from the open window. I crawl out of bed and shut it. The curtains tickle my arms as they flutter around me, but I am not in the mood for pleasant night air. These dreams are getting more intense, and the door that Sunni wants me to open is so close, yet so far. If I even want it at all, I don't know. How important it is to finding Joseph G. Campbell and defeating the Collective, that's the real question.

Sunni—the real Sunni, not the Sunni I conjure in my dreams—told me that she'd foretold my coming to Sparkstone in a dream, and that I am to play an important role in the events that will transpire here. Her power to predict the future in her dreams was so powerful and probably feared by the Collective that it became her demise.

A thought strikes me as I sit back down on my bed. What if the Sunni in my dreams is more than just an image? What if…what if it's the real Sunni, from beyond the grave?

I shake my head immediately to rid myself of the thought. Sunni is dead. She had the power to foresee the future in her dreams, not actually communicate through them.

Right?

Maybe it's the room. Her presence is still here, even though Ms. Agailya's staff cleansed every inch of the room and removed every item that belonged to Sunni. Instead of a blue-green glow from a luminescent fish tank, and soothing blue and turquoise tones on the walls, a rich olive colour that complements my eyes covers the room, and my instruments take up most of the space not filled by the nightstand and the dresser. The room is repainted and filled with different furniture and belongings, but that doesn't take away the feeling that Sunni still lives here, in an intangible, not-ghost-like way.

I turn over the dream in my mind. Something is going to happen on Saturday. In the library? I've never been inside Sparkstone University's library, and it's not underground, unless there's a part of the library that isn't open to students. Campbell's book—part of his soul, Sunni had said—a metaphor, or real? The dream-Sunni wanted that book, desperately. And if it contains information about Campbell, then I must find it as well. I'll decide down the road whether to share with Jadore in exchange for my father's life.

I held that book in my hands. There must be a way to find out if it's real.

I sigh and lean over the end of the bed to pick up my laptop, which is lying on the floor, then settle it on my lap. The light from the screen burns my eyes as I bring up Google. *Joseph G. Campbell,* I type. I feel silly typing his name into a search engine. Google shows me what I expect: "Did you mean *Joseph Campbell?*" The results are mostly bookseller links to *A Hero With A Thousand Faces,* as well as a handful of links to Facebook and LinkedIn profiles of guys I'm fairly certain aren't a mysterious being with an ever-changing face.

He chose his name well.

That, or, he can control technology, like Wil.

Right, Wil. He could probably use his supernatural talents to help me. His brain could surf the Internet faster than I could.

I close the laptop and sigh. Then again, even if Wil could find something in the bowels of the Internet, what then? How am I supposed to trust the information? What am I supposed to do with it?

I look longingly at the bathroom. Night is the best time to read Sunni's journal. But I'm afraid to take the risk. Joseph G. Campbell's note was clear: the journal must be kept safe. The note and the journal were delivered the day after she died, when the professors were cleaning out her room. This room. I'd hastily flipped through it in a steamed-up bathroom in case there were cameras, and when I moved into this room I hid it in the toilet tank and secretly hoped that I would forget it was there in case the Collective could read my mind as easily as it could see into the private places on Sparkstone campus.

I slip off the bed and tiptoe to the bathroom. The door creaks slightly as it opens and closes again, disturbing the thick silence of the dorm, and I stare my newest hobby in the face: fishing things from toilet tanks. First, though, preparation. I turn on the hot water in the shower. The mirror steams up, and soon it's almost as hot as a sauna in the bathroom. It's not a foolproof plan, but the steam might block a camera lens, maybe, if there's one in the bathroom.

I roll my sleeves up, carefully lift the top of the tank aside, and get to it.

Once the dripping wet plastic bag and its dry contents are safe on the vanity, I wash up thoroughly and dry my hands as best I can in the humid room. It's time to read.

I sit on the toilet and skim the pages of Sunni's dream journal. I wouldn't call stealing away to the bathroom to read Sunni's journal a nightly ritual, but it's pretty close to that. Mad scribblings and sketches, that's what most of these pages contain. The ones I can decipher are poetic, and I could probably spend days reflecting on them. I don't have days, though. Any more than an hour in here and whoever watches the camera feed outside the bathroom might get suspicious.

Dream-Sunni told me I have all I need to find Campbell's book. Trouble is, I've been over most of Sunni's journal already, and because there's so much crammed into each page, it's hard to find something that I have overlooked. I flip a few more pages and am running my index finger along the pen scribbles when I notice a page that's been carefully dog-eared. Curious, I flip to the marked page and scan it carefully.

I almost miss it. Sunni's small handwriting is interrupted by a curt, clearer cursive in the bottom left corner.

Campbell's Multiple Verses, Vol. II in library. Ref # 13042-4826

I think back to my first tutorial with Sunni, Misty, Jia, and Wil. Sunni had talked about finding a footnote on a website that mentioned one of Campbell's books, and that she and Jia had looked for the book in the library and hadn't found it.

My finger shakes as it hovers above the reference number. Not only had Sunni really found a book by Joseph G. Campbell, but she had also lied about it to Jadore. And it's right under the Collective's nose. I don't know if this reference number is for a book in the regular library or this mysterious dream library. Whether the Collective is aware of the book's existence, and has scoured the library to find it, I also don't know, but if my dreams contain an ounce of truth, then I am willing to bet that the Collective has not uncovered this book.

At least, not yet.

Saturday, September thirteenth. Perhaps I have until then to find it.

I close the journal around my finger to mark the page, and pace the small, hot bathroom. Why send me one book to lead me to another book? Why not just send me *his* book?

Maybe it didn't exist in the library until now.

I shake my head of these thoughts, rest the journal on the vanity, and undress. Sunni discovered the location of the book in her research or dreams but couldn't access it. I have to find out if there is an underground library at Sparkstone, break in, and retrieve what neither a fortune teller nor an omnipotent being could get for me.

Great.

CHAPTER 4

The library is one of the most-trafficked areas of the school, besides the cafeteria. A set of double doors in a building next to MacLeod Hall encloses a quiet buzz of mental activity. Pages flipping, whispered, heated discussions about philosophers and controversial ideas and project deadlines, and the persistent tapping on keyboards make me feel like I'm at a real university and not a prison for brilliant minds waiting to be harvested by aliens.

After my shower the previous night, I'd texted Jia and asked if we were still on for the meeting that Wil wanted to call. Jia told me she'd fought to get a private study room in the library. They're booked weeks in advance, and there are only five of them for over twelve hundred students. Fortunately Wil's technological persuasion skills came in handy, and Jia's name "accidently" knocked off a group of psychology students and got on the computer's booking form for the next morning.

I arrive in the library ten minutes before the Sparks to scout the place out. Unfortunately, the Sparkstone

University Library looks nothing like the library in my dreams, but I guess that's not a huge surprise. The main library is a maze of bookshelves, communal study areas, a computer lab with twenty computers, and of course, the main checkout area. A mechanical arch spans the width of the double-door entry, preventing students from taking books without checking them out. That could put a damper on my book-stealing plans. Just another wrinkle for Wil to smooth out.

Venturing to the back of the library, I see another set of doors. These ones block a darkened corridor. Large glass windows are set within the doors, and the left-door window is covered in multiples of the same paper sign: RENOVATION ON SATURDAY. APOLOGIES IN ADVANCE FOR NOISE DISRUPTION.

Bingo.

I peer through the right-door window to get a better look, and then try the elongated door handles. Locked. Above the door, in boldfaced serif, is: RESTRICTED SECTION. An engraved sign on the wall to my right reads: *Authorized personnel only. Special pass key required.*

I quickly let go of the door handles. I wonder if they record DNA, just like the other door handles in the school. I'll have to talk to Wil about getting a special pass key, assuming he can conjure up one for me before Saturday.

I finish navigating the bookshelf mazes in the main library and make my way back to the front, where Jia is waiting for me. She gestures to a private study room furthest from the checkout desk. "We're in here. Where were you?"

"Am I late?"

"No, not really. Wil and Misty are already in there though."

"I was just exploring."

I follow Jia into the private study room, and with a wary glance around, she shuts the door after us and locks it. The room has a single hanging lamp that creates dark shadows in the upper corners of the ceiling. Wil and Misty sit at a rectangular table—Wil at the head, Misty at the left rear. She's leaning back in her chair, her muddy boots up on the table as if she owns the place. Jia takes a seat to Wil's left, and I take the one to his right while casting a disapproving glance at Misty's muddy boots. If you're going to have boots, you have to take care of them.

"This won't take forever, right?" Misty says. "I have a paper to write."

"It shouldn't," Wil says. "So I've been tinkering with our new wristbands."

He pulls back his long-sleeved shirt to reveal the silver band. Each of us acquired one on our adventure a few days ago in space. I shake my head, trying to rid myself of the image of Sunni being struck down by Jadore's lightning powers. The wristbands we'd stolen from the alien shuttlecraft that took us to the mother ship had kept us safe from most damage, and they'd hidden our faces as well. Not that hiding our identities matters much anymore, now that Jadore knows pretty much everything about us.

I find it extremely suspicious that we found the bands in the first place. I think they were placed in the shuttlecraft— somehow—by Joseph G. Campbell.

"Can you fix them so that the gross gel doesn't cover our entire bodies like a one-piece wetsuit?" Jia asks.

"Can you actually figure out how to get these damn things *off*?" Misty adds.

Wil laughs. "Not really. That would take a *lot* of tinkering." He runs a finger along the sleek silver. "But I've managed to interface with the alien technology and make it more controllable. No more button mashing to get it to remove part of the gel covering. Just one button to press." He points to a small blue button on the band's tiny panel. "More importantly, though, I programmed a useful feature that I'm actually using right now."

He grins and holds out his hands proudly, as if we're supposed to give him a round of applause. Jia smirks and giggles. Misty raises an unimpressed eyebrow.

"What?" I ask.

"This library room wouldn't be safe for us to talk in normally. There aren't cameras, but there's a hidden wire under the table."

Jia gasps and ducks her head beneath the table. I look too. I don't see anything initially, but Misty feels the underside of the table, and I see her black fingernail move over a protrusion—a little knot in the wood.

"Yeah, that's it," Wil says. "I sensed it coming down the hall. So I activated this baby"—he gestures to the wristband—"and that's one less mechanism I have to worry about. Frees up my mind to concentrate on the actual conversation."

Misty crawls into her chair and perches on the seat. "Very clever."

He nods. "Glad you think so. It's playing a pre-recorded conversation between Jia and me. So that it's not so suspicious."

"Won't it look suspicious if it's just you and Jia talking, when Misty and I are here too?" I ask.

"No cameras, genius," Misty says. "Remember?"

"No, but the librarian saw four of us go into the room."

"Whatever. They'll just assume the two of us are quiet mouses, takin' notes about whatever their conversation is about."

"Mice. Two quiet mice. Seriously, you're a language major."

Misty scowls. "You're gettin' on my case about my major again? Miss Recites-Textbooks-At-Aliens?"

Wil throws up his hand. It's funny how such a simple action can silence the two of us. Maybe it's his mind power, maybe it's just his natural presence, or maybe it's because he's the only guy in the room. Whatever it is that abruptly ceases our conversation, it also glues our attention to Wil.

"Glad you guys are done arguing about p's and q's," he says. "Because there's something else I need help with."

"What's that?" I ask.

Wil leans forward, one hand resting carefully on his wristband. "I've been watching the trucks."

"Trucks?"

"Yes. Two white trucks, every Wednesday and Sunday, early morning, no later than nine, roll up Sparkstone Boulevard. They go towards the research facilities."

Misty leans back in her chair and tips it until it teeters—she could fall at any moment. "And you're tellin' us this because you have nothin' better to do on those mornings?"

"No, I'm telling you because these trucks are carrying a particular ingredient that goes in the drug, which goes in the food. The whole reason we avoid the cafeteria in the first place."

I sit up a little straighter. "The drug that made me sick."

"How do you know the trucks contain the ingredient?" Misty asks Wil.

"About a week or two ago, one of those white trucks came to our lab by mistake. The driver was new, apparently, got the wrong building. Most of us didn't care, including me. The head scientist in the department directed the guy to the right place, but he was mad. The head scientist is part of the Collective, so I'm always careful around him. Something about the way he handled the driver really piqued my curiosity. Especially because I never saw the driver again."

"Are you gonna get to the good part of the story?" Misty asks.

Wil throws Misty a look. "It took me a few weeks, but I finally figured out the truck schedule. And it was only a few days ago, after some creative hacking, that I found out what was in the trucks and why it was so important, and more about the drug in the food, which apparently the Collective casually calls Gen-Grow."

Jia smiles and leans forward. "Right. That was when we snuck into Building B."

I frown. Building B is one of the three massive research facilities adjacent to the field. "When did you guys do this?"

"A few days ago," Jia replies. She slides her gaze to Wil. "You didn't tell them?"

"No, I...I didn't want to until I had a chance to analyze the substance." He pulls a small test tube, no bigger than my pinkie finger, from his jacket pocket. It's filled with a green gel that has the consistency of toothpaste. "Colloquially, it's called Substance 454. Rare stuff. I've only seen it in a couple of science journals, and it seemed like science fiction until I saw it for myself in the labs. It's distilled from a whole list of stuff, but the important thing is that this is what makes Gen-Grow so, well, we'll say addictive. Everyone looks forward to getting food from the cafeteria, right? It makes you feel good. Relaxed. But at the same time, it makes you want more. Even smelling the food makes you crazy. That's Substance 454 at work. It's like someone put a whole bunch of oxytocin and caffeine and dopamine into a pot. It really is the ultimate feel-good drug. And wicked controlled too. Man, if this ever got out on the streets..."

Jia clears her throat, and Wil realizes he's ranting.

"Right. Well, anyway, it's made in secret in a facility somewhere, and then shipped here. Must cost the Collective a fortune to have people get it up here, though. Pretty sure I read that it's only processed in the States. I had Jia steal some bread and croissants from the cafeteria, and I cross-referenced the chemical makeup—"

"Hold it. You're an engineer. How'd you do any cross-referencin' with any kind of chemical without access to a bio lab?" Misty asks.

"We also broke into the lab on the second floor in the Conrod Building," Jia says. There's a hint of pride in her voice, and muted excitement.

"Well. Seems you two have been busy," Misty mutters.

To be honest, it was a good distraction...from Sunni, Wil admits to me—though whether he is speaking to me privately, or to all of us at once, I don't know.

"So the Collective ships Substance 454 here because they're creating the drug locally?" I ask. Wil nods. "I guess that makes sense. Is there anything we can do to stop the shipment of that ingredient?"

"That's the next step of the plan," Wil says.

"You actually have a plan?"

"Well, maybe. I'll need your—"

"Shouldn't we...I don't know, vote?"

Jia and Misty look perplexed. Wil frowns. "Why?"

I fall back into my chair. "Well, we're supposed to be like, a team. Right? Shouldn't we decide together how we're going to hit the Collective, and not just go and do things randomly?"

"Says the girl who tried to escape the other day? Without us?" Misty says.

"That was different. Jadore was playing mind games with me. I thought I could win. I underestimated her. I learned my lesson." I grind my teeth.

"The collection of this substance was not *random*. It did take a lot of planning. But I suppose if it would make you feel better, voting..." Wil adjusts his glasses. "I assumed it would be the best course of action. Gen-Grow helps to control the students, to keep them euphoric, to keep them from leaving the school. The most logical way to hit the Collective is to sabotage their drug supply, as it would cause the most damage."

"Fine," I say. "But I think we should consider other ideas before we go and break into other buildings. We don't want more of Jadore's wrath."

Wil considers me for a moment, and then nods. I wish I had his mind-reading abilities. Misty just shrugs, and Jia looks a little disappointed that I've curtailed their breaking and entering spree.

"There's something I wanted to bring up too before we vote on stuff," I continue. "It's about Joseph G. Campbell."

Misty rolls her eyes. "Not this guy again."

"Yes, this guy again. Remember how excited Jadore was when Sunni said she'd found information about Joseph

G. Campbell? She mentioned that he had treatises. I did a Google search and couldn't find anything about anything he might have written."

I've got Misty's attention, but only because I've brought up Sunni. "She knew about Joseph G. Campbell because of her dreams," she says.

"Yes. She was researching him the week that she . . . died." Misty squirms in her seat, and Jia looks sympathetic. "She said she'd found a reference to a book in the library about him. She almost admitted it to Jadore in the tutorial, but you, Jia"—I point to her—"came to her rescue by saying you didn't actually find it. And Jadore believed you, I think. But turns out there really is a book in the library, in the restricted section."

"I . . . I had no idea," Jia says, the tops of her cheeks reddening. "We really did search for a while. I was just trying to help."

"I know. But the problem is, the restricted section is being renovated on Saturday. The books down there will probably be moved or destroyed."

"Then how do you know Campbell's treatise is still there?" Wil asks.

I haven't told them yet about Sunni's journal. Nor have I told them about my dreams. I'm afraid that they'll mock me for thinking that Sunni is trying to tell me something. I'm afraid they'll dismiss me for claiming to have a superpower that Sunni once had. I would never want them to think I was replacing their friend. Wil had said not to write down anything about the Collective, in case it was discovered. Sunni had clearly violated the rule and paid with her life for her journal. Either way, I had to toss them a bone, to convince them I was confident that Campbell's treatise existed.

"I've been having these weird dreams lately," I say, drawing in a deep breath. "They're extremely real. Sunni's in them. I'm walking towards a door in a big restricted library section, and she keeps telling me to go through the door in whatever form it takes, but…but I can't, I always wake up or I die or Sunni dies again."

Jia looks contemplative. "What do you think it means?"

"I…I don't know. I want to think it's a coincidence, and I don't want to suggest it, but…"

"You think she's still alive," Misty whispers.

The idea scares me, because it rings true. I *did* hear a voice that sounded like Sunni's just before I teleported off the mother ship. And her presence in my dreams feels so real. If there's such thing as mutants and aliens, then it's not such a stretch to believe in ghosts.

"Maybe not alive, not in the way we think of life," I say. "But, maybe—"

"We watched her die," Wil says, waving his hand as though the matter is final. "I *felt* her die. I couldn't sense anything from her moments after Jadore's lightning hit her."

"But maybe her life force was too weak for you to sense," Jia says. "Just because her body stopped working doesn't mean—"

Misty leaps to her feet. "Stop this. Ain't no point in gettin' our hopes up. If she were alive, she'd be here, with us, sayin' that she could hear us."

She is so confident that I don't want to point out the potential error in her logic and start another argument.

"Maybe your powers are manifesting themselves in different ways," Jia suggests. "Teleportation, and communication with those who have passed on to the next life."

Misty grits her teeth. "I don't wanna hear any of that Buddhist crap where Sunni's concerned, Jia. Sunni…Sunni is gone. She's not some butterfly or a newborn baby out there somewhere."

"I didn't say it was probable," Jia replies. "Since Ingrid feels that her communication with Sunni is real, I was just offering possibilities."

"Well, I don't want to talk about this anymore." She sets her furious gaze upon me again. "So these *dreams* told you that the restricted section is being destroyed on Saturday? And they showed you the location of the treatise?"

"Not the exact location. I have a reference number…written down." I slide my gaze to Wil, who looks on in disapproval. "Well, don't expect me to remember long strings of numbers like that. Come on."

Wil can't read specific thoughts, but I'm sure he knows I'm not telling him the whole truth. Instead of calling me out on it, he looks pensive, and rubs his chin. "Restricted section will be tricky to get into. Especially if we have that time restriction."

"We'd need permission to get in there," Jia adds.

"Since when does the invisible girl care about gettin' permission to go places?" Misty asks.

"Since the restricted section of the library installed motion sensors last month," Wil replies.

Motion sensors installed a month before "renovations"? That's a clear sign that the Collective is hiding something important in there, whether it's Campbell's treatise or something else entirely. "Can you disable them?" I ask.

"I can try," Wil says. "But I can't disable them from outside, I don't think. I'll have to mod the bracelets to emit some sort of ray. That might be the easiest solution.

And we'd need a distraction. The library is open nearly twenty-four hours a day. It's only closed for a few hours in the early morning. And you saw how packed it is this morning, and it's only a Tuesday." The wheels behind his eyes are turning. "There might be something to that protest idea you had yesterday, Ingrid."

"Use the protest as a distraction to break into the restricted section. That could work, I think. Wait. What if... what if we were to protest the cafeteria food?"

"Everyone loves that stuff, though," Misty says. "No way people would rally against that."

Wil nods reluctantly. "Agreed. That would be hard to garner support for."

"Maybe it doesn't have to be specific," Jia says. "General frustration about lack of freedoms within the school might be a valid enough protest."

"But not everyone feels like they're trapped," I say.

Wil rubs his chin. "Gen-Grow could have a hand in preventing students from feeling frustrated."

I raise an eyebrow. "Can it do that?"

He shrugs. "Maybe. But if we were to somehow remove the drug from the food, at least long enough for people to wake up and start realizing that things just aren't fair around here, then maybe, maybe, we might have a chance at succeeding and keeping our hands clean." A small grin spreads across his face. "So we can move forward on my idea after all. Mess up the shipment of Substance 454, and hopefully the Collective will assume the faulty batch is a fluke. The students wake up and realize the injustices of the campus, the protest happens, and we sneak into the restricted section to steal Joseph G. Campbell's treatise before the Collective shuts the place down." He looks at me pointedly. "Everyone wins."

Jia looks less than convinced. "We can't be associated with the protest," she says firmly. "If it gets back to Jadore that we planned it, she could make good on her promise and harm our families."

I nod, thinking about how Jadore already has my father in her green scaly clutches.

"One of us will have to manage the protest while the others sneak into the restricted section of the library," Misty says. She drives her nail through a set of initials long-ago carved into the wooden table. "I guess I might as well volunteer. Jadore already thinks I'm a troublemaker."

Jia shakes her head. "No, none of us can be involved. It's too easy to trace it back to us. You'll get *transferred* like Sunni. I think I have a better idea. I know this girl." Jia wrings her hands. "She works in the psych lab with me sometimes. Her name is Laura. I think... I think she's also had some trouble with Jadore and a few other professors in the past few months. She keeps asking for permission to interview particular people for her studies, like child psychologists not affiliated with the university, and she's even asked to visit certain child therapy sessions in the province, but she's always turned down. Even phone interviews are restricted, and this makes it hard for her to choose projects she wants to do. Last week she got so frustrated that she told me she wished she could complain to the president of the university, Mr. Oliver Dean, but he's away on 'business.'" Jia curves her fingers into air quotes. "She was close to confiding in me about how unfair she's being treated, but then our professor came in and she couldn't say anything else."

"What's your point?" Misty says.

"My point is that if we need someone to be a figurehead for this protest, she might do."

My eyes are round. "Wait. You're saying that we should *frame* her for the protest? That if something goes wrong, she gets blamed?"

"Would you rather your father be killed?" Jia asks. "Jadore was clear with her warning. If we interfere with their operations here, we will be taken away as Sunni was taken away, and our families will be put in danger."

"I'm not going to put someone else's life in danger, no matter how little I know her." I rise from the table. "I thought we were supposed to be protecting the students here, not sacrificing and using them whenever we want. We do that, and we're just like the Collective."

An awkward silence descends upon the room. Wil taps his fingers against the table—*tap, tap, tap-tap*—the rhythm of my panicking heart. "I agree with you, Ingrid. But if we cannot protect ourselves, then we cannot protect the other students. Not everyone can be saved."

I am fuming. *Not everyone can be saved.* As if we have the right to determine who can live and who gets to die, just because we're aware of what Sparkstone is really about.

Wil's words trigger shadows in my mind, images from my recurring nightmare: the mysterious Joseph G. Campbell observing Jadore eat my innards as if he is at a zoo and not standing on the threshold between the known and the unknown. Does he too hold people's lives in his ever-changing hands and grapple with ethical decisions, or is he so removed from it all that deciding that Laura should take the fall would be as simple as deciding what to wear in the morning?

Wil is waiting for me to reply, his dark brown eyes inquisitive. Analytical. Jia's feelings are written all over her face. Her eyebrows are turned upward in an expression of sympathy, but they're also pleading. She wants me to say it's okay to put Laura's life in danger, because if it were her sister in danger, and not my father, she would have no qualms about risking an acquaintance's life for blood.

"I can't be part of this if that's our stance on casualties," I say. And then I eye Misty, who hasn't said a word since the debate began. "What do you say?"

Her gaze pierces me as her blue irises look up from the wood. "If it means we can get revenge on Jadore, then I support using Laura or whoever else to get what we want."

It's the final blow. I thought Wil and Jia had their heads screwed on right. But the three of them taking such a callous stance on this—I guess I was wrong about them.

"Fine. You guys can break into buildings and organize rallies. You're already doing a bang-up job without me. I'll find out Sunni's secrets on my own."

Misty snorts. "Yeah, with what superpowers? Good luck with that."

"I've gone eighteen years without superpowers and I've done just fine until now, thanks."

Although it's Sunni's dreams and her journal that have gotten me this far with my investigation.

I push that thought from my mind as I storm towards the door.

"Ingrid, please don't go," Jia says. "If you could just listen—"

I pull open the door. "No. I'm done. Just leave me alone."

"Bitch," Misty mutters as I leave the room. And then, louder: "We don't need you anyway! Good for nothin'—"

I let the door slam. If they think I'm good for nothing, fine. I know I'm good for something, and I don't need superpowers to prove I have worth.

⌒◉

I don't know where to go, but my feet do. I'm walking towards the Lewis Art Building. Sparkstone has a small jewellery and blacksmithing department, but the majority of the art students seem to be painters, both physical and digital. At least this is what Ethan told me, in one of our few treasured conversations.

Ethan. My stomach clenches and an anxious red-and-white ball of energy swirls within me. I will have to think of an excuse for bothering him at the art studio in the middle of the morning, assuming he's there. *Oh hey, Ethan, yes, I was just on a little walk, and* ... No, that won't do. Too obvious that I went out of my way. *Ethan, hey! Jia and I are organizing a school event and we were wondering if you wanted to do posters for us* ... Better. Though I really don't want to associate myself with them right now. Besides, if there are cameras in the studio like there are everywhere else, then there will be a record tying us to the protest, if it ever actually happens.

My time for thinking of excuses is up. I stand before the art building. The outside doesn't look much different than the other buildings at Sparkstone—brick, three storeys, double-doored entrance. The door handle buzzes in my palm as I pull it towards me. Scanning my DNA. Apparently the building finds me suitable enough to enter, as no alarms go off. Once I'm in the lobby, I inspect my palm. No signs of any pinpricks. It didn't take my blood this time, thank god.

76

The lobby of the art building is intimate. A young woman with dreadlocks and a blue and white scarf around her neck sits at a paint-stained reception desk a few paces from the entrance. There's an elevator behind her, and a closed door to my left hides a narrow hallway, probably full of offices. To my right a mural has captured the wall. It's Earth in two-dimensional form. My stomach lurches because I have seen this view before, in real life: the unforgiving blackness of space closing in on the blue and green and brown sphere that is Earth. The sun's yellow-and-white glow envelops the horizon and casts half our planet in shadow. The artist, whoever he or she was, nailed the essence of the scene almost perfectly.

I am so captivated by the mural that a light tap on my shoulder startles me. I jump out of my skin, only to realize it's the girl from the desk, now standing next to me.

"You need something? Someone?" Her accent sounds American, maybe from North Carolina.

"Um..." My eyes flirt with the elevator. "Yeah. I was just wondering if I could visit someone. If he's here. If it's not a bother."

She gives me a look that tells me she thinks I'm crazy, and then walks around to her desk again. "Canadians. You're not botherin' me. It's my job. Who're ya lookin' for?"

"Oh...his name is Ethan. Ethan...Millar?"

"Sure. Ethan. Yeah, he's upstairs. Want me to buzz him so he can come down, or were you here to see his art?"

I feel like a fish out of water. My mouth opens and closes and opens again. "I'm here to see his art."

"All right." She scribbles on a piece of paper, and then hands it to me with a pen. "Sign where the *X* is, and then sign out when you leave."

Another layer of nerves piles on to my already nervous stomach. Now, a physical record that I visited Ethan will exist. But that's not suspicious. Ethan is my friend. I am here to see his art. I sign my name as lightly as possible on the allotted spot and pray that it will magically get rubbed away by the elements.

That done, the girl gestures to the elevator. "Third floor. Second door on the right."

I smile at her gratefully and press the call button. The doors slide open immediately. I hide in the corner of the elevator after pressing the appropriate button. The doors slide shut and for a moment, in the tiny space, I feel safe. The air is a little musty, but the smell is comforting. It is the scent of my favourite sweater, and the old church halls in Cape Breton draped in tradition and memories, where weekly dances are held. No tiny red eyes in this space, watching me. For a moment I relax. A jaunty jig plays in the back of my mind but escapes when I try to catch it. Maybe this visit is a good idea. I could use some inspiration. Writing music will help me forget the atrocities I have seen, and will see again.

The elevator dings and the doors slide open. My boots touch down on a glossy wood floor. It's lined with scrapes and years of wear, but it smells as if it were laid yesterday. Light browns, emerald greens, fairy forests—I see and smell these colours, these images, more intensely than ever before. I'm not sure whether it's the creativity that lingers in the building that's infecting my brain or if it has something to do with Gene 213 or whatever it is awakening inside me, but I can't stop the associations from firing in a million directions between my ears.

Second door on the right is open. A tin whistle echoes in the narrow hallway, and I peek into the studio. There are three areas in the room, partitioned only by the multiple canvases hanging on the walls. Each shows off a different art style—one, brightly coloured abstracts, another, detailed portraits of naked women, and the third: fantasy landscapes and women warriors fighting dragons. It's here I find Ethan, painting a woman in a flowing blue dress looking into a pool of endless depths.

I stand in the threshold watching him. A vein sticks out prominently from his forehead, and he has a crease between his brows—he's concentrating, he's in another world, trying to capture the look of this mysterious woman in the painting.

Maybe this visit was a bad idea. I'm not that mad anymore. I should go back and apologize to Jia and Wil and Misty and try to work something out with them. Or I should go work on my own project before Jadore finds out I've been slacking off.

As I turn to leave, the music fades. The tune has ended. My boots *clomp clomp clomp* on the wood. Ethan makes a startled sound behind me, and there's a rustling of papers and a clattering of somethings falling to the floor. I spin around. Paintbrushes roll at his feet, and sketches float like snowflakes around him.

"Ingrid," he says, surprised.

I wave. "Hi."

I've completely interrupted his painting session. I rush to help him pick up his things.

"Oh, no Ingrid, that's all right, I didn't even hear you come in, you don't have to..."

But I've already got a fistful of paintbrushes in my hand.

Some of them are wet, some of them have paint on them. Blue splatters on my fingers and my shirt, but his eyes are locked with mine, and that makes it worth it.

"You're all right?" he asks.

"Of course," I say quickly. "Why?"

"Oh. I just mean, I saw you yesterday. You looked upset. What happened?"

My face heats. "Oh. You were there... outside?"

"I was just heading back to my dorm for a second for some extra supplies, and I saw Jadore on the steps of Rogers Hall, and thought I'd better get out of there quick 'cause I didn't want to get in trouble for missing my meeting with Ms. Agailya, but then I caught a glimpse of your hair..." He stares at my long, frizzled locks momentarily, as if taking in their inherent beauty. "There were a lot of maintenance men around you too. Did you break something?"

The hafelglob seem to like maintenance overalls, that's for sure. The image of their creepy, slimy tentacles wrapped around wrenches, trying to fix something broken, is almost funny. Almost. "No, um... they were just..." My brain is the thing that is broken. I'm struggling between *Oh my god Ethan is looking at me* and *How do I come up with a believable excuse?* "Escorting me."

"Escorting you?"

"Yes." I sigh. The truth is probably the best thing I could offer him right now. Or at least, as much of the truth as I can admit without attracting Jadore's attention. "I'd just... learned... my dad's in the hospital."

Ethan's jaw falls open. "Oh, Ingrid, I'm so sorry."

I purse my lips. "Yeah. Um, car accident."

"So..." Ethan frowns. "Why were those men escorting you?"

Great. Dig myself another hole. "I guess I went a little...crazy."

I can never look sane around him, can I?

I feel the heat of his hand on my arm, and his fingers are sticky with paint. There is sympathy in his eyes. "If I found out that someone I loved was in the hospital, I'd probably go mental too."

My chest constricts. The truth is in the sob welling in my throat, but I force it down. I'm staring at the floor again, at Ethan's brown laced shoes. Would he be able to handle the truth? He must suspect that something is wrong with this university. If Jia is right about the whispers in her lab, and if Wil is right about the food supply being laced with a drug that makes us complacent and awakens Gene 213, surely he must have heard something about it?

I try to be tactful, and bits of the truth fall out of me. "I'm not even allowed to leave to see him. They almost took my cell phone away, just because I was being too loud, and I guess I was screaming. Some of the rules here are really unfair."

"Yeah, I noticed cell phone coverage is bad up here. 'Course, it costs a fortune for me to call home, so I try not to use cells too much."

I purse my lips again. He didn't even nibble that conversational bait. Time to be more direct. "I mean, not just cell phones, Ethan. Haven't you noticed all the heavy security here?"

He seems to think about it for a moment, and then shrugs. "I guess. To be honest though, Ingrid, I've never been to North America before coming to Sparkstone, and I thought this much security at a prestigious university was normal. Sure, it's definitely annoying, but they do some top-secret research here, so it's only to be expected."

My jaw drops, but he's right. A secretive university would demand high-security measures. But maybe Gen-Grow prevents him from thinking too critically.

He sees my surprise and then grins, lopsidedly. "Hey. You planning on doing something you're not supposed to? That why you're testing the waters here?"

I'm taken aback. "What?"

"I'm not stupid. You trying to scale the gate? The wall?" There's a mischievous twinkle in his eye, and this combined with his accent makes him pretty much irresistible right now.

"Scale the gate? It's...it's awful high," I reply. "And not doable in my boots. I think if I were to rebel against the university, I would do something a little more...achievable with high-heeled boots."

"Something that you need my help with?"

My heart beats a little faster. I clutch the neck of my shirt. "I...well..."

"That is why you've come here, right?"

Now I'm the one being tested. My immediate instinct is to deny the flimsy reason and cut right to the chase: tell him how I feel and tell him the truth behind Sparkstone so that we can protect each other. But he's thrown me a lifeline because he's right: why else would I run to him?

I smile coyly. "Well, there could be something you could help with. Maybe."

"Oh?"

The colours in the paintings surrounding me give me an idea. "It's not a sure thing yet. If it happens at all. But if it does happen, we could use your artistic skills."

He raises a curious eyebrow. "Who's we?"

"Me and my..." The word *friends* is on the tip of my tongue, but we're fighting now, and so it's weird to refer to them as people I like and trust. "Just some of the people I hang out with."

"Using my art to instigate a rebellion. Sounds..." His smile widens. "Sounds risky."

"It could be." I lose some of the lightness in my tone. "I don't know. Forget it, I should really—"

The floor creaks behind us. "Hey, Ingrid!"

Oh. It's Kimberly. She breezes into the room, her silky, flowing cardigan trailing behind her like a superhero cape. Her face lights up when she sees Ethan, and she squeals in delight even though it probably hasn't been more than a few hours since she's seen him last.

"Hey, you," she says to Ethan in a low, sexy voice that I'm not sure if I'm meant to notice. "Glad I caught you here. Evergreen Café is closed today. But the bakery is open. Maybe we could get a bite there?"

"Evergreen is closed?" I ask. Never mind the fact that she's asking him to lunch. "Why?"

She blurts out my fears. "Okay. Well. This is just a rumour, but I heard that someone got food poisoning."

"Don't you and your friends eat there a lot?" Ethan asks me.

I nod, but my mind is reeling. So Ohz was telling the truth. Or, some variation of it. Maybe the food had always been infected with Gen-Grow, and someone was finally reacting to it. "Do you know who got sick?"

Kimberly shrugs. "Dunno. Glad it's neither of you, though. Or me. The nurses here can really overact and drug you up good if you complain of even minor stuff, like headaches. I used to have chronic migraines when I was in high school—okay, okay, it was because I used to drink a lot of energy drinks and stay up all night painting. Rinse and repeat for five days in a row, blah blah blah— but when I came here and had to paint for like, deadlines and stuff, and I went to the nurse to get some Tylenol because I had run out, she kept me in the infirmary for *hours*! Pricking me with needles, doing blood tests, pee tests—anyway." She finally takes a breath. "Suffice it to say, I don't go to the infirmary anymore, I've cut back on my caffeine intake, and whenever I feel a headache coming on, I just tie a bunch of pillows around my head and continue painting."

"I've seen her do it," Ethan adds, smiling.

God, she has a mouth on her. The *will we, won't we* feeling that had swelled between me and Ethan has evaporated like water in unbearably dry heat. Ethan places his paintbrushes on the rainbow-stained table next to his easel and scrapes remnant blues and greens from his fingertips with his nails.

"So, uh, lunch then, at the bakery?" he says.

The way he says it, it sort of sounds like an invitation. Kimberly nods eagerly, grinning at Ethan, and then at me.

I can't return her enthusiasm, so I examine the girl in Ethan's painting more closely. She does look a lot like Kimberly. He used her as one of his models. I was supposed to be one of his models, before I had to go into space to try to rescue Sunni.

There's a soft rapping on the door frame, and then Wil's voice fills the room. "There you are."

More people, intruding on Ethan's space. I see a tension in Ethan's eyebrows as his gaze lifts to Wil. "Oh, hey, Wil."

I shouldn't be surprised that it's Wil who has come for me. His power led him here, to this sacred place of art, where his mathy, technological brain has no place being. But I turn to face him because it's polite. Wil is not looking at me. He's returning Ethan's stare. Stepping into the room, one large shoe covering two planks of wood that creak under his stature, he's got this look on his face, as though he's the one being intruded upon. It's almost as if Wil has claimed this space with his mind, and everything in it—the paintings, the easels, the stained tables, and the three of us as well.

"What are you doing here?" I don't mean for the question to sound indignant, but the anger of our earlier meeting rises like vomit in my throat.

"Just looking for you," he replies, just as curt. He lifts his hand in a wave to Kimberly. "Hey."

She returns his wave with ten times the giddiness. "Hey! Haven't seen you in a little while. How's your project coming?"

"Oh, uh..." Wil hesitates, like he wasn't expecting Kimberly's friendliness attack. "Good, I guess. Yours?"

"Great, great, great! Tell you about it later, okay? Unless you want to come to lunch?" Her eyebrows lift with hope.

He shoves his hands into his pockets and shakes his head at the floor. "No, no, I, uh, already have plans with Ingrid actually."

"Oh really," I say icily just as Ethan asks, "Where you going?"

"Making sandwiches. We're going to have a picnic," Wil says. He looks at me expectantly. He wants me to participate in this lie so that I will talk to him. Telepathy isn't needed to convey that.

Kimberly grins. "That sounds amazing! I wish I had've thought of that. But I, um, don't want to interrupt. We'll go, before the bakery tables get filled up." She tugs on Ethan's arm.

She *doesn't want to interrupt*. Was she fishing for an invitation? For herself, and Ethan? "Maybe—"

Don't, Wil warns. His voice is powerful and loud in my brain, like my ears are plugged and his G minor tone is all I'm allowed to hear.

But Ethan catches my words. "What's that, Ingrid?"

Please, don't. We can't have you mad. Put their safety first and talk to us. We're ready to listen, Wil pleads.

I draw a deep breath. Had they reconsidered using Laura? No, they couldn't have changed their minds that quickly. Jia was set on the idea.

The three of them are waiting for my response. I nod once, quick and sharp, to Wil, and sacrifice my personal life once more for the safety of the students at Sparkstone University. "Oh, nothing. Go ahead, Ethan. You two go ahead." I hate saying it. I hate giving him my blessing to go have lunch with her, not just because of the green jealousy that twists and turns in my stomach, but because now I feel that Kimberly is one step ahead of me when it comes to winning Ethan.

"All right," Ethan says, and there's a layer of disappointment in his voice.

Kimberly hears it too. "Ethan." She punches him playfully in the shoulder. "Don't pressure the poor girl. You *are* taking her out on Friday, aren't you?"

My breath hitches. She knows about that. Of course she does. I wonder what else he's told her. What they do together when they're alone. What their relationship really is.

Stop it, I tell myself, but my mind is spinning. I don't know where I stand anymore.

Wil squints at me. I hadn't told him or Jia or Misty about my date with Ethan. This was not how I wanted them to find out. I scamper toward him and the door.

Ethan mumbles something to Kimberly and then looks at me apologetically. "I'll see you later, Ingrid."

I savour the sound of my name on his lips. As Ethan draws out his keys to lock up the studio, Wil marches out the door and down the hall, in the opposite direction of the elevator. He doesn't want to be stuck with them on the ride down, though that was my last hope of stealing secret glances at Ethan for the day—the torture of seeing Kimberly and Ethan together and imagining what they say when I'm not around would be worth it.

"Bye," I say, pressing myself against the door frame before tumbling out into the hallway. Wil is nowhere in sight, but turning the corner, I see there are some back stairs. The elevator dings distantly and Kimberly is yammering away—loud, then softer and softer until elevator door closes.

I'm alone again. For a moment I contemplate breaking into Ethan's studio and spending hours poring over his paintings, looking for any clues about him or his life or his thoughts about me or Kimberly or anything. I'm almost crazy enough to do it. My feelings for him, this vicious infatuation, it consumes me, and I spin around.

"Ingrid."

Nope, can't escape. My boots scuff on the hardwood in protest as I skid to a stop. "Wil, I really don't feel like—"

"We really do have sandwiches made for you. Jia said that ham and mustard was your favourite."

I heave a sigh. That's true. I told her that a few days ago when we went shopping at the market. We could afford only one condiment, and she was going to buy the ketchup. But I had reached for the mustard. My dad really enjoys mustard, and we would always layer our sandwiches with it at home. Sometimes I'd forget the meat, and only have bread and the mustard. Mustard sandwiches, my mum would say, and laugh. I'd told the story to Jia casually, and having no preference herself, she replaced the ketchup on the shelf. That she had remembered this small detail about me in a sea of other information was strangely...intimate.

I pivot around slowly, my arms crossed, and silently follow Wil down the stairwell.

CHAPTER 5

"We can make this work," Wil says firmly. "What do you think?"

We're picnicking near the field that stretches beyond the campus. The field ends abruptly at the large concrete wall that surrounds the town—keeping us all in, and unwanted humans out. At least there aren't any cameras out here, as far as we know. I eat my mustard and ham sandwich quickly, eager to fill my mouth with food rather than talk about what had happened this morning in the library, and in Ethan's studio.

The protest will be held on Thursday evening, two days from now. We'll stay for the first ten to fifteen minutes, and then one by one, except Wil, we'll slip out and meet at the library. Jia will get us into the restricted section with her invisible-girl powers, and the alien wristbands we stole from the Collective will neutralize any electronic security, with a little tinkering from Wil. Then we'll search for Campbell's book there.

But to make the protest legitimate, we first have to hijack the trucks that carry the ingredient that makes the poison that goes into the cafeteria food. That way we can make sure that whatever effect the poison has on the students is lessened, and we can expose the truth, hopefully, during the protest. Or rather, Laura can expose the truth, since the protest, unfortunately, will be hers.

"I can protect her," Wil assures me. "I know that using an innocent student as our mouthpiece makes you uncomfortable, but between my power and the wristband, we can make it through this, keeping Laura safe and the four of us anonymous. The Collective won't show its true face and risk blowing its cover in front of all the students. However, if Jadore arrives and begins abducting students, I can plant a suggestion in her head that Laura is innocent. But I'd have to be physically close to her to do that. And"—he heaves a heavy sigh—"if things get hairy, I might be able to convince everyone to leave, maybe even forget that the event happened in the first place. That would take a lot out of me, but if I had to, I would do that."

I hate that it comes down to this. I hate that I have to rely on Wil and the others to use their powers to make this work. I bite down on my bottom lip. I don't want anyone else to die. But I have to trust Wil if I want to strike the Collective secretly and keep my father alive.

"Even if you're able to work your mojo on this girl, won't Jadore automatically blame us anyway? She *suspects* our genes are ready to be…harvested," Misty says.

"That is always the risk. We could be harvested tomorrow," Wil replies. "We can do nothing and wait to be harvested, or we can go down fighting."

"No one should have to die," I say.

"Like I said. I'll do my best to protect Laura and everyone there while you raid the library." Wil picks at the grass beside the blanket. "It will also give me the opportunity to spot any emerging Sparks."

"Maybe you'll find that Laura is one of you," I say.

"One of *us*," Jia says.

I purse my lips. "Yeah. One of...us."

I know I'm part of the group. It's the first time in my life that I've felt part of something bigger than myself. But Wil, Misty, and Jia—and Sunni, when she was still alive—all had powers that they could control and use for a greater good. Me? I could maybe teleport if I concentrated really hard. Maybe.

"I just think tomorrow is too soon for this truck heist," Jia says. She sits cross-legged on the grass with her back perfectly straight. "We need more of a plan."

"We can't keep waiting for a better time," Misty says. "Strike now"—she flattens her palm against the blanket that she, Wil, and I are sitting on, and when she withdraws it, there's a blackened imprint of her hand there—"and we'll have a better chance of surprising them."

"Or Jadore will know it's us, and she'll kill us all," Jia replies. "And our families."

"If the heist is successful, they won't know we've tampered with the ingredient. At least they won't suspect until after the protest," Wil says.

"There are a lot of *ifs* supporting this," I say.

"A lot of *ifs* support everythin'," Misty mumbles.

I sigh and look Wil square in the eye. "You're sure that you can protect Laura if something goes wrong?"

"Yeah, I can," he says.

"And about planting the protest suggestion in her head, you're going to just...visit her dorm room one night and magically place it in a dream?"

Jia's cheeks flush. "I can take you, Wil, to the psychology labs to do it, if that is easiest."

"Yeah. I guess I'll take you up on that," Wil says.

I bury my face in my hands. "Do I have to go along with the truck heist? I don't see how I'll be useful there."

Misty dips the rest of her sandwich into a bowl of salsa. "You're the bait. The distraction, while we do the actual stuff."

Yes, of course. I'm sure Misty would love nothing more than to see me devoured by a hafelglob while she and the other Sparks save the day. Jia frowns disapprovingly at Misty.

"Fine." I look at my cell phone. It's nearing the middle of the afternoon, and I'd promised Ms. Agailya yesterday that I'd visit her office. I brush bread crumbs off my skirt as I stand up. "How early do we have to meet tomorrow?"

"Seven," Wil says.

Misty groans and plants her face next to her handprint on the blanket. "So early!"

Wil is not impressed. "The truck will come between eight and nine. We have to be ready."

"Where?" I ask.

"I'll let you know," he replies, pointing at his bald head.

Great. More relying on Wil to tell me where to go and what to do, but it seems as though I don't have a choice in this matter. I'll do my part to help in this war against the Collective—I just wish I could control my own power.

"You know," I say, folding my arms, "I think it's important that we meet Laura. She is a human being. She needs to be a willing participant in the protest—even if she doesn't know what she'll be taking the fall for."

Wil purses his lips and then glances at Jia, who hesitates but then nods emphatically. "I agree. Though I don't think she'll be unwilling."

That's what worries me the most. She might be willing to participate in the cause, but we won't be able to tell her everything.

Misty looks mildly bored. "Do we all have to meet her?"

"The fewer of us involved in this, the better," Wil says. "But if the Collective does get a hold of her and I don't act fast enough to erase her memory, they will eventually find out that we were speaking with her..."

"If they don't find out before that, you know, from all the *cameras* all over campus," Misty says.

"They don't have cameras in the little psych lab offices, I don't think," Jia says.

"Good," Wil says. "That's settled."

Misty jumps to her feet. "I hope that means we're done here." She's already speeding across the field, phone out, checking her messages.

"Tomorrow. Early," Wil calls after her.

She waves her hand at him dismissively.

Wil and I get up next so that Jia can gather up the blanket. "I'd better get back to work," she says. She turns to Wil. "You going to the Conrod Building?"

Wil shakes his head and sits back down on the grass. "I'm going to sit here for a bit."

"Oh. Sure." Jia waves goodbye to me and trudges across the green alone.

I'm about to follow when Wil's voice stops me. "Did you ask Ethan to do art for a poster?"

My stomach twists. "Not really. But kinda hinted at it, yes."

Wil heaves a heavy sigh. "You know that if we plaster the school with posters, and one of the professors recognizes his art, he could get in trouble."

Dammit. I hadn't thought about that. I had just wanted him to be involved so much that I didn't think of the consequences.

"I don't know if posters are a great idea, in any case," Wil says. "We only have a certain number of photocopier credits on our key cards. One hundred per semester, something like that. They notice that one student or more has used her credits up in one go, on a protest poster? That's trouble. I mean, I could bypass the system and convince the copier to use whatever card I want, but Jadore will be suspicious if there's no card number associated with the account. That will lead it back to us. Your father will be at risk. Unless... unless you want to use Laura's card."

I grit my teeth. "I suppose that's the whole point. Getting her to take the fall."

"I've already promised to protect her." Wil climbs to his feet and towers over me. "What else do you want from me, Ingrid?"

I gulp. I'm tall, but he's half a head taller. "I just want to make this as simple as possible."

Wil snorts. "I shouldn't even bother asking you what you want."

He brushes past me and starts back towards the dorms. I whirl around, mouth agape. I march after him. "Excuse me? What's that supposed to mean?"

"You know what it means. You want Ethan," he mutters.

"So? What's that to you?"

He stops and pivots. I'm afraid of his gaze now, because

I don't want him to admit that he has some hopeless crush on me. I don't want that to ruin our growing friendship. I don't want to lose someone else during this war, when we're supposed to be working together.

Wil stares at me for a long moment, his expression cracking and exposing more soft torment of feeling with each second that passes. "Nothing. I'll find a way to get Laura's code number for her photocopying credits. I'll see you tomorrow."

Ugh! I clench my fists with rage as he leaves. I hate this. I wish I had his power, instead of a stupid non-functional teleportation power. Then I'd know exactly what he's thinking, and what Ethan is thinking.

I gather my things and run for Rita House. It's time I have a little chat with Ms. Agailya.

∽

"Thank you for coming in, Ingrid."

Ms. Agailya rises from her desk as I step into her office. The walls are painted a baby blue, and paintings of sailboats and ocean waves crashing onto rocky shores adorn the blank spaces between the bookshelves. She gestures to a cushioned seat in front of her desk before returning to her black leather office chair.

"I'm here to, um, solidify my majors, I guess," I say.

"Of course." She opens a drawer in her desk and pulls out a form. "What subjects are you interested in pursuing?"

"Psychology," I say quickly.

Her pen glides across the page as she fills in one of the boxes. "And your project this semester—why don't you describe it for me, briefly, for the form?"

An involuntary sigh escapes me as I lean back in the chair. "I'm studying theoretical physicist Joseph G. Campbell's theory about multiverses, travelling between multiple existences, and the potential effects on the brain."

Ms. Agailya turns her calming gaze up at me. "Have you given thought to how this will tie in with your second major?"

"No," I reply quietly.

"Well," she says, bending the form up slightly, "there are many routes you could go with an ambitious project like this. Do you have an interest in physics?"

I shake my head. "Not really."

"Neuropsychology?"

"Moderately."

"Astronomy?"

My breath catches. "Maybe. What would astronomy have to do with Joseph G. Campbell and multiple universes?"

I feel like I've caught her in a trap. Ms. Agailya settles the form on the desk and laces her long, delicate fingers. "The multiverse theory is largely considered science fiction among theoretical physicists. If you wanted to approach it from that angle, you could elaborate on the effects of space travel on the human brain, and how this travel may equate to travelling between dimensions."

"But travelling between dimensions isn't the same as travelling between universes." My posture straightens. For the first time in weeks, I feel as if I'm in my element. "A dimension is kind of like the volume of an object, and its place in time. That's not a very good explanation, I know. It's oversimplified. There are the three spatial dimensions that we use to express positions in space, and of course, there's time—and a whole bunch of other constructs to express various mathematic ideas that I barely understand. But a universe is…well…it's the place where these dimensions operate." I lean forward to punctuate my argument. "You seem to know a lot about Campbell, for a university admissions administrator."

"It is dangerous to define a person by her profession."

"What do you know about him?"

"Ingrid, you—"

"I don't want to pretend," I say. "I just want to talk. And maybe I'm wrong, but I feel like you might be the kind of person who will listen."

She shakes her head sadly. "Ingrid, I am not the only one listening. You know this."

"Yeah, I know. But you've put me in this prison, and you've asked me to dance. If I don't dance, more people could die. So what choice do I have, really?"

"You can choose to be silent. You can choose to not pursue this topic."

"I'm too far in now to go back on any decision I've already made." My hands find my hips. "This was what Sunni was secretly working on when she was *transferred*. If there is anything you can tell me that might help me in my research, I need to know it."

"I do not know anything, Ingrid."

There's a collection of pens in a holder on the desk, and I'm so frustrated I feel like flinging it across the room. I clench my hands to control my impulse. "How can you stand by, knowing that innocent people are being *murdered*?"

Her pale, translucent gaze finds the camera I've been

looking for. I resist turning my head to see it, somewhere above the door.

"Everyone has different reasons for joining the Collective," she replies. "Scientific advancement is our primary objective."

"And you achieve that goal by murdering young girls?"

Pain twists her face. "The Collective is not one mind. I wish that could have been avoided."

I grip the edge of the desk as I stand. "So do her friends."

"What are you planning, Ingrid?"

My face pales. "Nothing."

She grimaces. I don't think she believes me. I'm not a great liar. Leaving right now would just prove to her that we are up to something. I curl my toes in my boots and count the seconds of silence until she speaks again.

"Whatever it is you are planning to do, please, do not." Ms. Agailya rises, and slides around her desk. "My people have a saying. Translated, it means, *Do not make waves in water you do not intend to breathe in.* I assume I don't have to explain that to you."

I consider her words. "I don't want to make waves here. I just want to do what's right for *my* people."

Her smile is sad and wise. "I fear that it is impossible to do what is right and not make waves."

She's right, I know. I nod slowly, and my heart sinks. "I just thought..."

"I know." She averts her gaze. "I cannot do anything for you at this time about this matter."

I frown and think about what Misty and Wil and Jia said earlier. They had asked for her help and got nothing. It was stupid to try, maybe. A waste of time.

Ms. Agailya skirts her desk and picks up a pen daintily.

"I will leave your second major blank for now, Ingrid. Please think carefully about it and let me know what you intend to study as soon as possible."

Yeah, I'll get on that, between sabotaging some chemicals and staging a protest and stealing a book from the library. I nod and pull open the door.

CHAPTER 6

I wake up to Wil's voice in my ear. *It's show time.*

No, it's time for me to go back to sleep, I want to scream. I was up half the night worrying about everything: my dad, the poor girl Laura, and of course, my project, which I have done zero work on. Like a zombie I shuffle into the shower, and it does nothing to alleviate the growing bags under my eyes. After applying heavy makeup to conceal my lack of sleep, I text my mom. And then I call her. But nothing. Just her voice mail.

My meagre breakfast does nothing to help my nerves: two sesame snaps, my last apple, and two glasses of water from the sink. Hell, I shouldn't be drinking the tap water—it's probably full of the drug we're about to sabotage—but if I don't stay hydrated I'm afraid I'm going to die.

Wil's voice filters into my mind about a half hour later. *You ready? We'll be in the field.*

My boots are a must, as usual, but I opt for skinny jeans for this mission, as it's getting colder outside and running in skirts is no fun. I choose my least-favourite shirt, in case of hafelglob slime, and my rain jacket, in case of downpour. Grey clouds gather over the campus, and I wonder if Jia's invisible world is permeable to rain.

I sigh and rearrange my hair in the mirror. I settle on a long braid, which reaches down the left side of my chest. "You can do this," I tell my reflection.

I leave five minutes later after locking my room and stuffing the key card securely in my jacket. Passing the communal bathroom—not sure why we have these, as I was under the impression that most rooms had a bathroom suite, but maybe not—I hear girls complaining inside about a variety of things: the early hour of their tutorials, individual meetings with professors, and their project. I gulp and rack my brain for a ready excuse as to why I'm up early, in case I am confronted.

Already the walls are lined with our handiwork: a poster advertising a school-wide meeting in the cafeteria on Thursday. Tomorrow. I made something really simple in a word processor, all text, no images. It includes information about the location of the protest and states that the quality of the food in the cafeteria is being called into question. In the computer lab in MacLeod Hall, a place that many students in a variety of faculties use, Wil was somehow able to retrieve Laura's code from photocopier, and he made over a hundred copies of the poster. Jia put them up all over campus while in invisible-girl mode, again aided by Wil and his masterful and deft control over the cameras.

Three girls exit the communal bathrooms and point to the posters. "Oh yeah, I heard about that," says one. "We're going, right?"

"I don't know. Sounds kind of boring. And lame. The food is fine here. Great, even," says another.

"I heard that some of the professors were taking the posters down in MacLeod Hall," the third girl whispers. "Maybe it's some sort of conspiracy."

They disappear into one of the dorm rooms and I hear nothing more. Anxiety swirls in my stomach. I hope to god that Wil knows what he's doing with this ingredient. We need proof that it's affecting the students, and we only have a day to come up with that proof. Today has to be successful if we are to have any chance convincing the students that something is very wrong at Sparkstone.

Out in the field, the grass is dewy and wet and smells as though it's just been mowed. Wil and Jia are already there. Jia is dressed in capri yoga pants and tank top. A headband holds back her slick black hair. Judging by the sweat gleaming on her forehead, I'd say she just finished her daily morning run.

Wil wears a navy Harvard hoodie with light cargo pants, and I almost laugh at his silent protest. He was supposed to go to Harvard, and had just arrived in Boston for an orientation and tour when Sparkstone agents greeted him and *kindly escorted* him to a private jet plane that brought him here. Needless to say, his parents were pretty mortified, and no doubt Harvard administrators were confused. Or dead.

"Did you see Misty?" Wil asks as I approach.

"Good morning to you too," I reply. "And no. She's not here yet?"

Wil folds his arms and looks out over the town. "She's getting worse. I don't know what to do with that girl, I really don't. She's still in your building, moving slower than molasses."

"She's really not taking Sunni's...transfer...very well," Jia says as she stretches her calves.

"You don't have to be a mind reader to know that," Wil says. "But she's better at hiding her feelings than most. Even from me. But that's just because of—" I think Wil realizes he's talking out loud and grits his teeth to stop talking. "Anyway. We don't leave soon, we're gonna miss our window of opportunity."

"I can go get her," Jia says.

"No, I just yelled at her. She's running now," Wil replies. He checks his watch. "We'll be cutting it close. Maybe I'll just go on ahead. Better if we're not all travelling in one big group anyway."

"We have me, though," Jia says. "We can travel together using *me*."

"Yeah...I think I'll just go on ahead to make sure"—he stops— "oh, wait. Here comes Misty."

I spin around, and yep, there she is, a black dot growing bigger by the second as she runs across the field towards us. She looks more dishevelled than usual. Even though her personality is rough around the edges, and her clothes are full of holes, her hair and her face are generally immaculately groomed. But not today. Her hair flies all over the place as she runs. She smoothes it down as she skids to a stop before us. Dark eyeliner envelops her eyes as usual, but its application looks rushed.

She shoots me a challenging glare as I evaluate her appearance. "What?"

I purse my lips and return her gaze. "Nothing."

"We should go," Jia says. She takes in a deep breath and closes her eyes. Misty holds out her hand as if the action is a chore, and Jia takes it. She holds out her other hand to Wil, but he shakes his head.

"Ingrid and I will go together. You two stay out of sight for as long as you can."

Jia glances back and forth between the two of us, and then nods slowly. Something flickers on her face: jealousy?

Wait. *Does Jia have a crush on Wil?*

It's at the forefront of my mind as Jia and Misty shimmer and disappear into Jia's invisible realm. And knowing Wil, I assume he can probably see exactly what's bothering me.

He waits a few moments, presumably to give Jia and Misty a head start, and then gestures to me. "Let's go."

I follow him silently. I can barely keep up with his long strides as he takes us down a residential street. Presumably it's a quicker way to the front gate. This early in the morning, the town of Sparkstone is just waking up. Men and women kiss their spouses goodbye on identical front porches as they leave for work. Most of them probably work in the labs on the campus. Others might be professors—whether or not they are human or alien, I can't tell. Others still are shop owners. I wonder if any of them are parents, if their children are waking up in the dorms at this very second, if any of them have been threatened or harmed because of actions their children have taken against the Collective.

Wil stops at the end of the street. Before us is the road, surrounded by an expanse of flat plains, which leads out to the gate. He takes me into a backyard, neatly mowed, and we duck behind a wooden fence. I gaze up at the household.

"They're not home," Wil says. "This is as close as I can get without being seen."

"We could've gone with Jia and Misty."

"It's better if we are not together."

In case we are caught is the unsaid part of that sentence. Fine. "Are they close?" I ask.

"Jia and Misty? Yes. They're nearing the gate."

"That's...that's good." My legs are getting tired of crouching, so I kneel on the grass beside a shrub. Wil sits cross-legged across from me, staring at the fence as though he has x-ray vision and can see through it. For all I know, he could have this power.

I hear no traffic on the road, so the supply trucks haven't come yet. Or, they've come and gone already, and this whole mission is a bust. I heave a sigh and my thoughts turn to Ethan. I make up a detailed scenario in my mind where Jadore crashes the concert this Friday and I'm forced to fight her off to protect Ethan. I smile a little at this, even though the scenario is ridiculously dangerous. I just want Ethan in on our secret. Maybe then I could go on missions with him, and it could be Ethan sitting here with me, instead of Wil.

I try to think of a way to broach the subject with Wil. "Do you think that—?"

"If you don't mind, I don't want to talk about that right now."

I'm taken aback. "Oh. Um, all right then."

He falls silent, mentally and physically. He's a machine, the wheels behind his eyes turning, fixed dead ahead on the mission just a few feet away.

And then, a thought, innocent as cupid's arrow piercing my heart, strikes my mind. *What if Wil has a crush on me?*

It would explain his odd look when he caught Ethan and me talking to each other. And Kimberly had given me this look—half blush, half knowing smile—as if she and Wil shared a secret. Wil had mentioned that he and Kimberly knew each other—does he know her well enough to confide in her? He has helped me a lot in the week since I've been at Sparkstone. But that could just be because we're friends.

Ugh. I'm hopeless at having guy friends. I cannot tell the different between flirting and friendliness.

I wrap these thoughts up in a box and store them deep within my mind, but I have no doubt that Wil can sense what I'm thinking. He straightens his glasses and peeks above the fence again.

About fifteen minutes until the supply truck comes, Wil says to my wandering mind.

I nod.

See there? He indicates the toll booth with a bowed head. *The truck may stop here for inspection. But Ohz and the guards, if they know the truck driver by sight, may just wave him through. I will open the gate for a few seconds for Jia and Misty to get through, and hold it closed for as long as they need. Hafelglob don't have the same brains we do, but he is in human form, so I may be able to influence Ohz to stop the truck if we run out of time, but only as a last resort.*

"That's your plan?"

Wil raises an eyebrow. *Yes. You're the real distraction, in case I can't get him to stop.*

Lovely. "I'll do what I can."

"I know," Wil whispers slowly, using his mouth and not his mind now, for reasons unknown. "Jia and Misty are in position."

On the other side of the gate, I see two maintenance workers—probably human, but maybe not—smoking, and Ohz, reading something in his cramped booth. A camera stands vigil on top of one of the gate poles, its red eye surveying all.

"Do you think they have heat sensors in the cameras?" I ask.

Wil grimaces. "Not yet. But if they find out about Jia's power, installing some will probably be the first thing they do." He closes his eyes and cocks his head, listening, perhaps communicating with Jia and Misty. I hear his voice in my head once more. *We don't know much about the Collective, but what we do know is it's an organization with a budget. I worry about their technology, and how fast it grows, but in the tech lab I sometimes hear them arguing—just like human scientists argue when they don't get funding for their projects.*

I wish we didn't have to worry about these things. I see it in his face. We're first-year university students. We should be worrying about exams, and our careers. It wasn't that long ago that I graduated from grade twelve, where these worries were paramount. I'd once told one of my school friends that in five years, I saw myself playing in prestigious concerts, starting my master's degree in psychology, and publishing papers about the mysteries of the human brain. Now that my future seems intertwined with the fate of these other three mutants, and the fate of every student at school, I don't know where I see myself in five years. It seems that I may not even make it five days into the future.

"All right. You should get going," Wil says. "It will be Misty and Jia's responsibility to get them to open the back, but it's yours to keep the truck stalled for at least five minutes so they can get in and out."

"Okay."

"Good luck, Ingrid." He smiles grimly and, to my surprise, lays a reassuring hand on my wrist. *It probably doesn't seem like it, but I have faith in you.*

I rise slowly to my feet and allow his hand to fall naturally. My stomach is fluttering with his faith—if that's what it really is. My legs are stiff from the tightness of the skinny jeans and the tall boots combined, and the crouching and sitting didn't help either.

I have faith in you. The memory of Wil's voice echoes in my ears as I take off towards the gate. When have any of my friends ever said that to me? My parents always say they are proud of me. But that's not the same as faith. Faith implies I can do something even though it may not be actually possible. I've only known the Sparks for a little over a week. They barely know me—and yet, this unwavering faith, this faith that I am indeed the person whom Sunni predicted would be the key to the Collective's plans at Sparkstone, this faith that somehow I can control the clandestine power within me, this faith that I won't screw it all up—I actually believe him when he says it. He means it when he says he has faith in me.

Despite my hesitations about having secret powers and getting involved in an alien-human war, despite my fears about my family's safety, I've always wanted this. I've always wanted to be part of a greater cause. To give my skills and talents meaning in a world that after high school becomes so confusing and easy to flounder around in, lost. To have people who will catch me if I fall.

I must not let my friends down. I must not let my family down.

I'm almost to the gate when a truck tears up the road.

I pick up my pace. No, wait. Two trucks. Oh no. How do we know which truck has the ingredient? Do we need to sabotage both trucks to be successful?

I glance behind me, wondering if Wil can sense my panic.

The gate parts slightly of its own volition. That must be Wil allowing the invisible Jia and Misty through so they can get to the trucks. Ohz leaves the booth and flags down the trucks. Now I'm sure the other two "maintenance" workers are hafelglob, because I can see that the cigarettes they're holding aren't even lit. They watch the trucks coming in casually, as though they're two normal dudes with nothing better to do.

Well, here I come to give them something better.

One of them frowns as the gate opens and closes, but the trucks pulling up seem to put any suspicion out of his mind. The truck drivers cut the engines. A strange silence settles over the open expanse. One maintenance worker goes around to the back of the first truck with Ohz, presumably to inspect its contents. The second notices me running towards the gate and hails Ohz.

"Girl with the flame hair, she comes!"

My stomach heats and boils at his clumsy speech, but it's too late, I'm committed now.

Ohz peeks around the back of the first truck, and his face brightens when he sees me. This face of a forty-year-old man, with forehead lines of a man twice his age, teeth of a chain smoker, and voice of a foreigner fools most. According to what Ohz was all-too-willing to admit to me when he broke into my bedroom a week ago, they are promiscuous as well. That was more than I wanted to know at the time, but maybe I can use it against him today.

We approach the golden gate with matching apprehension. Only a dozen golden bars and a mechanical lock mechanism stand between him grabbing me and returning me to Jadore.

"What is Crosskey doing back at my gate?" There's a salacious look in his eyes that makes me question my presence.

Ohz isn't going to buy this. He knows something's up.

He slips closer to the gate and wraps his sausage fingers around the thin golden poles. "Is Crosskey going to attempt escape? Crosskey cannot run faster than Ohz. Though...Ohz does like the game of chase." He grins his smoker's-teeth grin, and I shudder.

"That's not why I'm here," I say. My words are measured. Calm. "I'm here because I have information for your *mistress.*"

"Crosskey wants to meet with Mistress, she can do this on her own," Ohz says. But he sounds uncertain.

"I could meet with her on my own, but then what would you have to gain from that?"

Ohz presses his face against the bars. Indented lines criss-cross his skin, and the gelatinous nature of his true form shines through and hugs the metal. He turns his large eyes up to me. "Explain, Crosskey."

Here comes the tricky part. I just need to keep him talking long enough for Jia and Misty to sabotage the substance. "You were kind enough to warn me about your mistress' temper a few days ago. I didn't listen. And now my father is..." My voice breaks, and I let it happen. Anything to be just convincing enough to keep Ohz's attention away from the truck. "Look. I just thought that I'd return the favour. But, if you think that I should meet with your mistress directly, then I should take your advice, since, well, since you were right the last time."

I turn and wait a beat. And then I shuffle away. *One one-thousand. Two one-thousand...*

"Crosskey, no go."

One of my boots scuffs the dirt as I shove my hands in my pocket and look over my shoulder. I successfully hide a smug smile.

He turns a wary eye to the twin trucks. The two maintenance workers—alien—board the back of the second truck. Hopefully Jia and Misty had a chance to jump in there too. "Crosskey come back later. When Ohz is not working."

Shoot. He totally suspects something's up. I can't lose my cool now.

I run my front teeth across my chapped lips. "Um, well, all right." I have to keep talking. "I just thought you were always working. I didn't know you had breaks and off-times."

Suspicion fades away and something replaces it—sympathy? "Mistress is kind to Ohz. Allows his people good life while working on Sparkstone Project."

Sparkstone Project? I shudder. That's all this university is, a project, a test tube. And Jadore being compassionate? I can't picture that either.

My hands become fists as I steel myself once more. "I guess once the Sparkstone Project is over, then, your people and your mistress will be on their way, back to...wherever you come from."

The alien in human disguise sticks his ear through the space between the golden bars. "Crosskey is being nice to Ohz today. Crosskey not trying to run again, is she?"

"No, Ohz, I told you. I...I learned my lesson."

The first truck starts its engine again, and one of Ohz's co-workers goes for the booth, to open the gate. I draw a sharp breath, but Ohz doesn't notice my alarm. He's gesturing to the alien in the booth, telling him to hold up. Then he joins his co-worker in the booth. They seem to be fiddling with the controls—Wil's mental hold on the gate is firm. Jia and Misty must not be finished in the trucks yet.

The other maintenance worker comes around the side of the second truck. And the gate, it creaks as it parts. Jia and Misty must be waiting near the entrance to get through.

Oh no, no, no, no, Wil says to my mind. *Jia and Misty are still in the truck! And I can't—*

My eyes widen. The gate is opening. Wil's supposed to be in control! What is going on?

Jia and Misty are stuck in the second truck! I've lost control of the gate! Do something! Wil yells.

The gate doors are splayed wide. For a brief, split second, the prairies and the Rockies lay before me. Nothing stops me from running. I could...

The first truck rolls towards me, and so I do the first thing that comes to mind: I throw myself in front of a moving vehicle.

"Crosskey!" Ohz shouts, bursting out of his booth.

The truck slams into my gut. It's not moving that fast but the force is enough to splay me across the dash. The surprised driver brings the truck to a screeching halt. Behind him, the second truck brakes quickly, and there's a gentle *clunk* as the contents shift in the back.

Ohz runs towards me. It's so strange to see alarm and

concern on his face, and for a moment I forget that he is not human. "What is Crosskey doing?"

I think fast. "You have to help me, Ohz. I don't have anyone else I can trust."

"Crosskey trusts her friends, no?"

"Well, yes, but this…this is different." I inch closer to him, one hand on the front of the truck for balance. "My parents are in grave danger, and I can't get in touch with them."

"What makes Crosskey think—?"

"I don't know!" I scream, and pull at my hair. The crazier I seem, the better. "You don't know what it's like. Being in this…this petri dish, being threatened, having your family threatened if you don't follow the rules. There has to be some way, some small way that you can find out if my dad is all right."

"Crosskey did not come here to talk to Ohz about mistress…?" Ohz seems to be piecing together the bread crumbs I've laid for him. "Crosskey…trusts…Ohz."

I don't want to get any closer to the gross, slimy, tentacled alien that's hiding beneath this facade of a human. I swallow my fears and my memories of his body odour as I creep closer. "I just want to know how my parents are doing. Can you help me with that?"

Good, they're getting out. Just another minute, Wil says.

"Ohz…Ohz does not know." His words are slow and deliberate. "Your personal communication device, it does not function?"

"I can't get through. I need to know they're all right."

"Well…" Ohz's gaze slides towards the town, and then back to me. "Ohz did hear communication this morning about Crosskey's family."

"Yes, what?" A cold rush of fear runs down my back. I'm not acting anymore.

"Crosskey's father...is in hospital still," Ohz says. "Not awake. But alive."

That's a relief. It could be worse. I clutch the V-neck of my shirt. "And my mother?"

"Ohz does not know about the mother. Only Crosskey's father was mentioned."

She's probably okay, I tell myself. *She's probably at Dad's side. Maybe she can't call because Sparkstone is blocking transmissions, or because she's busy juggling work and making sure Dad gets the best care.*

"Mistress...Mistress will not enjoy hearing that Ohz had conversation with Crosskey."

"I won't tell her if you won't."

"That...that pleases Ohz." He grins with his yellow human teeth, and I think about Ohz's real teeth, small and sharp, spiralling down his throat. He places a cold, clammy hand on my arm, and it lies there limply. "Crosskey should get out of way of trucks."

"Oh. Yeah." I carefully move my arm from Ohz's grip and step off the road. I look up at the truck driver, who has rolled down his window and is looking at me with a mix of alarm and relief.

"You all right there?" he asks with legitimate concern.

"Yeah, fine," I say quickly.

He mutters something about being thankful for not having to fill out any insurance paperwork and takes off quickly down the road. The second truck follows, and the driver waves to Ohz. Ohz doesn't wave back—he just nods his head, his whiskery chin resting just a second too long on his chest, as if this is his first time nodding to someone.

I glance towards the suburb, where Wil is hiding. "I should...go."

"Crosskey can visit Ohz any time. As long as Crosskey does not run out the gate."

"Right. I...I won't."

I haven't heard from Wil, so I don't know if it's safe to leave, if my distraction gave Jia and Misty enough time to escape, but all I want to do right now is get the hell out of here.

I back away from Ohz and the other aliens in disguise and take off running. I follow the road, looping around a random side street to hopefully throw off any potential tail, and then take a left onto the street where Wil and I were hiding. When I get to the end of the street, however, he's not there. A curse falls from my lips.

"Wil?" I call out tentatively, fearing who may be watching.

The air is quiet and still. The cookie-cutter houses, with their white shutters and their white siding and their greener-than-green lawns, they're mocking me with their perfection. Nothing is wrong with us, say the houses with contempt. We have no problems, because that is the way the Collective made us.

"Fine. I'm going back to the campus," I mutter, mostly to myself. "My friends better not be dead."

And then a hand suddenly grabs my wrist, and I'm pulled backwards into the thick world of the invisible.

I cough and sputter, and I blink—there they are, the three of them. Misty looks severely annoyed, Jia looks relieved, and Wil looks mildly embarrassed. It's Jia who has my wrist, who is keeping me in the watery world that is unknown to the naked eye.

"We should head back," Jia whispers to the rest of us. Her grip is deathly tight, and she takes the lead down the street. Misty and I have no choice but to be dragged along with Jia. Wil holds on to Misty as if he's afraid she's going to run away from him. Jia's invisibility can extend to a person or an object if she touches it, and if that person touches someone else, they can also be pulled into the invisible realm. So the four of us, we stride down the streets of Sparkstone, holding on to each other for dear life because we've got nothing else to hold on to, nothing to keep us afloat.

"What happened with the gate?" I dare to ask once we're close to campus.

Wil looks uncomfortable. "I'm sorry," Wil mumbles. "I...I got a phone call. Had to take it."

"And you couldn't just ignore it!" Misty says, while Jia asks, "From whom?" Apparently the two of them hadn't dared to bring it up before either. Stress can sometimes affect Jia's ability to stay invisible. Maybe they were just relieved it was over. I know I was.

"Kimberly Sharma. Asking if I...well, it doesn't matter now."

Kimberly? Why would she be calling Wil? I wonder selfishly if she's asking Wil about me and Ethan, trying to scope out the competition.

"I assume you got the job done?" Wil asks Misty.

"I melted the ingredient," Misty whispers. The tips of her fingers are still red from the heat. Wil gives her a stern look. "I didn't melt it that much. Just boiled it to the temperature you told me. Changed its makeup, whatever."

"And I took a sample, like you asked," Jia says.

"The workers, did they notice?" I ask.

Misty looks at Jia and then shakes her head. "Don't think so."

"One of them…one of them looked through me. I don't think he sensed anything," Jia says.

Wil seems to relax. "Good job, you two."

Jia's cheeks warm. "Thanks, Wil."

We tread in relative silence back to the edge of the campus, avoiding the highly trafficked areas. Once there, Jia releases us, one by one, back into the world of the visible. Her face is paler than usual—being invisible for long periods of time drains her, especially when she has to keep more than one person in her watery world.

Wil digs his phone out of his pocket. "I should head to the lab to analyze the new information right away. And work on my project due next month."

"You need any help with the analyzing?" Jia asks, hope infusing her voice as she digs into her jeans and pulls out a test tube of neon blue liquid.

"No, I'm good, thanks."

So that's the ingredient that made me sick, I think as Jia hands it to Wil. He pockets it casually. He waves and then he's walking away from us, as if we didn't just sabotage a truckload of dangerous chemicals meant to mess with our minds.

"Yeah, I'm outta here too," Misty mutters.

"Wait, Misty, did you want to go for a run with me?" Jia asks.

She shakes her head, draws her cell phone out of her pocket, and starts texting as she walks away.

Jia sighs. "How about you?"

"Sure," I reply, smoothing out my hair. "After tutorial?"

"Yes," she says. "I'd better head back to the lab to finish

my paper. You want to come with? Keep me company? Unless you have stuff to prepare?"

I cross my arms. A breeze lifts my hair in various directions before settling it around my shoulders once more. "No, I think I'll just take a moment out here."

She smiles. One of the reasons I like Jia the most is because she understands what I'm not saying. "Text me if you... if you want to talk about anything."

"Okay."

Jia runs in the opposite direction of Misty, and then it's just me. Another breeze picks up. Goosebumps ripple across my arms, and a surge of excitement builds within my chest. We just *did* something. Adrenaline courses through my veins. We're activists. Paragons of change. A triumphant melody soars through my brain and in and out of my ears—I must write it down and try it out on my keyboard. Maybe I could write an acoustic guitar part, just for Ethan! Yes, that would be another excuse for us to get together.

The melody carries me towards Rita House, up the stairs, and down the hallway to my dorm. I'm humming my victory song as I unlock and open my door, but the tune falls flat in my mouth, lanced with a final, deep note of fear.

My room is in shambles.

I slam the door quickly behind me. My mattress is half off my bed, my blankets discarded on the floor, the curtain rods falling off their places on the windows. This was more than just an accident. My dresser drawers have also been disturbed, and my clothes shifted. I wouldn't have cared if the Collective had just destroyed the furniture. It does not belong to me.

But my instruments do.

My instruments are extensions of my being. My children. It would have been better if they'd just taken them. But no. Lying against the wall, broken in half, is my harp. Splinters try to hold the pins in the neck together, but the strings have given up and fall limp in all directions, like sad spaghetti.

The red light of the ceiling camera is unwavering. Silently watching. Recording every movement.

I don't even want to turn around to look at my keyboard, so I do it quickly, and the pain of its wounds strikes me through the heart. My keyboard has been tortured, its keys plucked from their rightful places and strewn across the floor and the box spring.

Then, a third stab in the heart: Sunni's journal. In the bathroom. If they've taken it, we're done for.

Oh god. Please let it be there, please...

I nearly trip over the broken pieces of my keyboard as I clamber for the journal's hiding place. I stop short before the bathroom door and grip my dresser for support. That's what they'd want me to do, go straight for what they want. I press my forehead into the edge of the dresser, and a high-pitched wail escapes me. Only one, because I don't want them to see me like this.

I step towards the bathroom and stop before the partly ajar entrance, pretending to examine the vanity for damage—there's barely a scratch. I try to forget the massacre behind me. As I slip into the bathroom completely, my gaze falls to the toilet. My heart is in my throat. *Is the journal still in there? Is it...?*

I move the top of the tank aside and peer into the water. It's there. The Collective did not find it, and I'm willing to bet that Joseph G. Campbell had something to do with that. This is the second time he's saved Sunni's creation, my adopted child, but he did not save my children. The water bubbles expectantly and the plastic bag tilts and rises slightly towards me, as if asking whether it's okay to come out now. I replace the top of the toilet carefully. *No, no, it's not okay to come out, not just yet. Mummy has to clean up the remains of her children first. Go back to sleep and dream the beautiful pictures to match the words within you, while I get down on my knees.*

In the threshold between the two rooms, I sink to the carpet and tile. My throat is tight. *Why would they do this? Do they know what we've done to Substance 454? No, I've been gone an hour, and they could've used that time to stop us instead of ransacking my room and destroying my treasured instruments. So why?*

The answer is frighteningly simple: to show me who's really in control here. The more I rebel, the more I don't care about what I'm supposed to be doing, the more Jadore will turn her porcelain, uncaring face away and order the death of what I love. To succeed in this game, I have to be a robot, just as uncaring as them, and carry out my research and the purpose I'm supposed to have in the Collective's master plan.

That, or come up with my own master plan, and execute it with the same swift, unfeeling nature that they have shown me.

But I'm not unfeeling. No, I will not dismiss what makes me *me*.

I clutch one of the white keys and feel its undamaged smoothness between my thumb and forefinger. Although it has been torn from its mother, it is still whole. All of these pieces, scattered across my dorm room floor, they are pieces of something greater than themselves.

Then, a memory, Sunni's voice: *Don't you let them make you think that you're alone. 'Cause you're not.*

They want me to be as broken as the instruments before me. I can't give them that satisfaction, no matter how torn apart I feel inside. *Wil and Jia, and Misty. Mom, and Dad…and Ethan. Although I am away from them, I am still whole. Me and them together, we create something greater than all of us standing alone. I am still strong. I will make it through this day.*

I pick up the pieces of my fragmented keyboard and set upon uniting them.

CHAPTER 7

I decide not to tell the Sparks about my broken instruments. I'm worried that Wil and Jia will cancel our heist and the protest, and I don't want our hard work—and the sacrifice of my musical instruments—to mean nothing. Misty's reaction would only be salt in the wound, and I don't need that, not now. In the hour I have before tutorial, I collect the wooden pieces of my harp quietly and bravely for the camera and place them in my suitcase. I lay the piano keys messily in order. I wonder briefly if Wil can fix it, as it is a machine, but that would require telling him, and I cannot do that today.

Asking for Ethan's help is more tempting. I see it now: running to him like some damsel in distress, begging him to help me fix my instruments, using my musical tools as an excuse to spend more time with him. Even that leaves a sour taste in my mouth. It would be a brief respite from my grief, but it would not heal the damage that the Collective has done. Not really.

I change into a pair of yoga pants, my sneakers—stiff from not being worn much—and a tank top. I might get chilly in the classroom, but the running afterward and my burning anger should keep me warm.

I lock my door, even though I wonder if there's really any point. During my trip through the third floor hallway, down the stairs, and into the main corridor of Rita House, I am single-minded. Like I'm marching into battle. Too many people are sauntering down the hallway, and a voice in my head panics. I don't want to be late. The thought is enough to propel me faster towards the exit.

Once I'm inside MacLeod Hall, I hear the *thunk thunk* of her cane before I see her. Throngs of students make way for her seemingly blind stumble through the hallway. I glare at her, as each step she takes is measured. Beneath those reflective sunglasses, she sees me and she slows her march.

"Good morning, Ingrid."

I don't give her the satisfaction of my gaze, or my voice. Nearby students give her funny looks for her uncanny ability to know who is beside her. They have every right to be suspicious. Now, they just have to rise up and kill her so we can be done here.

Jadore tries again. "The morning is not so good for you, I know."

I grit my teeth and walk a little faster towards the classroom.

"Run if you like, but we know what good that does," she says with a laugh.

I hate you, I hate you, I hate you, you take everything I love and destroy it. Someday, I will destroy you.

My backpack and notebook are still in Room 216, thank goodness. Someone has propped them up in the corner of the room. I gather a pen and the notebook as the rest of the students enter the room—including Misty, Wil, and Jia—and Jadore takes her place at the head of the semicircle.

I sit and hope that my silence will make me invisible to Jadore, but she does not let up. Every discussion, she asks for my opinion. My brain cannot shut off, it cannot wander, even though it has never really left my dorm room. I parry each attack as best as I can. Some of the blows land me right in the stomach, and all I want to do is leave the classroom crying. But I bite the side of my cheek and remain.

"Because some of us insist on underperforming today, there will be an extra tutorial on Saturday at noon," Jadore decrees, thumping her cane. *"Mandatory."*

The hour does not pass quickly enough. I'm the first one out the door when the torture session is over. I shove my stuff in my locker, and my hate carries me outside, all the way through the campus until I hit the field that spans much of the back of the town. It's quiet here, and I stew in my anger for ten minutes or so until Jia shows up, ready in her running clothes. She stretches her calves and exhales deep, calming breaths, as if she is preparing for a marathon.

"Wil is busy in the lab, preparing for tomorrow," she says, even though I don't ask or necessarily care. "I thought you weren't going to come. Are you all right?"

"Fine." I start stretching with her. "Let's just run for a little while."

"Okay." Jia does not pry. She has the wisdom and serenity of a Jedi Master. A small part of me resents this as she leans to the side, her arms stretched and poised like a ballerina preparing to pirouette. I will have to tell her eventually about what happened to my instruments. I want her to press me about it. But I don't want to argue. I just want to run.

After a few minutes of quiet stretching, she raises her eyebrows in a silent question, asking if I'm ready. I nod. She takes the lead down the field. I follow. It's not easy getting into a pace that I'm comfortable with. Cross-country running has never been my thing. Sports in general aren't my thing, and that self-doubting voice makes excuses as I fight to put one foot in front of the other. We near the place where I woke up a week ago and thought I was dead. Jia's breathing contains a gentle rhythm that I try to emulate, but viscous cramps attack my sides. I grimace, but I do not slow my pace.

Jia seems to sense my discomfort. "You're not breathing right, that's why you're getting cramps. In through your nose, out through your mouth. Still too fast." Her instructions are friendly enough to be heeded but firm enough to be respected.

I alter my breathing and try to focus on the run. But every time I push thoughts of the Collective, and my broken instruments, and Ethan out of my mind, they come back with such a vengeance that I'm tempted to trip myself and lie in the grass, to clutch the earth and beg it to take me from this world so that I don't have to feel anything.

"Did you notice that Wil has been acting strange lately?"

Her question seems to come from nowhere. I frown and latch on to the distraction eagerly. "Well...no. I don't think so. But we've all been a bit out of touch."

"Yeah." We're near some of the research buildings now. She slows down, clutches a nearby tree branch to catch her breath, and presses her forehead against the rough bark. Then she slides her dark eyes to me. "Probably nothing, then."

I'm thankful for the respite, but I continue to move my legs so that I don't lose my building momentum. Her gaze unsettles me. Maybe I'm not the only one trying to run from a problem. I feel bad about lying to her, so I backtrack. "Well, there might be something."

"Oh?" Her eyebrows quirk playfully, but it's almost as if she's trying to look disinterested at the same time. "Tell me."

"This is just in my head. So you probably shouldn't tell anyone. Like Misty or anything."

A small smirk on her thin lips. "I don't talk to Misty that much. And Wil...well, I think he respects us all enough to stay out of our heads. I think."

I shiver as I remember the look he gave me when he found me with Ethan. She gestures to a footpath that winds around the research buildings, and together we set off running again. We run side by side on the narrow path, and Jia throws me nervous glances every few seconds, waiting for the response to her question. I gather my nerves.

"Jia, I think...I think Wil has a crush on me."

She skids to a stop. Tiny rocks fly from beneath her shoes and pelt us both in the shins.

"Why do you think that?" she asks, her voice strangely flat.

My mouth is sandpaper as I tell her about what happened in Ethan's studio. She listens intensely, fiercely, like a judge who's presiding over a trial. Telling the story aloud makes the whole situation sound lame. My evidence is flimsy at best.

She looks as if she's trying not to laugh, or maybe cry.

She starts running again, and I have to run faster to keep up. "Ingrid, he doesn't have a crush on you."

"Oh." I'm surprised at how relieved I am. I'm carrying enough weight on my shoulders with my feelings for Ethan—and his feelings for me—as it is. "So that was just nothing, then."

Jia squeezes her fingers together so tightly that her knuckles turn white. "Probably not, no. He wasn't jealous of Ethan going to lunch with you. He was jealous of Ethan going to lunch with Kimberly."

Oh. Oh! I crack a grin. This is too perfect.

Wil likes Kimberly. Not me.

My relief comes out in a nervous laugh. "Oh! Well... you're sure, right?"

"Pretty sure, yes."

"Would be pretty awkward if he did like me. I mean, he's nice and everything, but Ethan..." I draw in a deep breath to soothe the cramp twisting at my side. I've mentioned my feelings for Ethan to her before. "Hey, Jia, did...did...I ever tell you about when I kissed—?"

Jia slows down again. She laces her fingers on top of her head. "Are you tired?"

Even though I'm about to tell her about me kissing Ethan on the field, I'm half in my dream world again. "What? Oh, um, not really."

"I might run on ahead, if you don't mind."

"Oh. Well, sure. I guess I'm almost done anyway."

"I'll see you later, then."

She takes her earbuds out of a slender fanny pack around her waist, sticks them in her ears, and races off down the path, around the research buildings. I stretch my calves and watch her go, puzzled. Was it something

I said? Maybe she didn't want to hear me go off on a tangent about Ethan. Girls with obsessive crushes can be annoying.

Or maybe she didn't want to hear me talk about Wil liking Kimberly because I'm not the only one with an obsessive crush.

⟋⟍

We're not meeting with Laura until later in the afternoon, so I take the opportunity to go back to my room to do more research on the human brain. I hate returning to the scene of the crime. The temptation to bury my face in a pillow is strong.

My enthusiasm for brain psychology quickly peters out, and I find myself staring at a wall of text on Wikipedia. For all I know, my computer could be tapped or wired so they can tell exactly what I'm doing. It was still in its place under the bed when I checked after cleaning up my instruments, but I notice it's slower to boot up. Fortunately I deleted the poster files I'd created right after I sent them to Wil.

I pace my room, thinking of all the possible ways the protest could fail. It's tomorrow, and I'm afraid of a million things: Jadore calling for our deaths, students becoming so disinterested in what we—or rather, Laura—have to say that we will be no further ahead than when we started, Campbell's book being gone by the time we get to the library, making everything we've done pointless.

I can't stay in my room. It holds too many anxious memories—memories of Sunni, of my dreams, of my instruments. Five minutes before I'm due to meet Jia, I storm down the hallway. I'm not even sure she'll want to see me after our conversation this morning, but it's not as if she has a choice.

I'm almost to Jia's room when who should enter the hallway but Ethan. He's wearing a winter toque and his nose is rosy, though I don't remember it being that cold outside. Maybe he's just not used to Canadian weather. His eyes dart around the corridor and fall on the protest posters still stuck to the walls, and then they rest on me. I nearly stop, wondering, first, what I should say to him, and second, what he's doing on the girls' floor.

"Hey there," he says. His voice is raspy.

"Hey yourself," I say, slowing to meet him. Jia's room is just a few doors down, but now I'm in no rush to leave. "What are you doing here?"

"Oh. Um…" He takes a hard look at his surroundings, as if he hadn't realized he was in a corridor until now. "I…I guess I was a bit lost in thought. Came up here. Was visiting Kimberly. Your new room is on this floor, yeah?"

"Yeah, it's right down there," I reply eagerly, gesturing with my thumb. My excitement diminishes as his words hit me: *was visiting Kimberly.* I can't see them getting up to anything romantic in the state he's in, if that was his intention at all. Maybe he feels guilty for running into me, and that's why he's acting so weird.

An awkward silence ensues. Ethan sniffs and wipes his nose on the back of his hand, then seems to think better of it and pulls a tissue from his pocket and blows hard. I struggle for another topic, anything to prolong our conversation. The posters lining the walls come to my rescue. "So…you think you're going to go to the thing, in the cafeteria?" I try to sound casual about the probable disaster that will be tomorrow.

"Oh, um, I dunno." His face is pale, and sweat stains darken his armpits. The hair sticking out of his toque looks damp.

I want to comfort him. "You all right?"

Ethan clears his throat and wipes his brow. "Yeah, yeah, fine. Well..." He wipes his sweaty hand on his leg. "I guess I'm not a hundred percent today. A cold. I didn't get much sleep last night."

"Oh." I frown. "Want me to take you to the school nurse?"

"That bad looking, am I?"

"No!" I say, way too quickly. "I mean, you just look sick. That's all. I...I just don't want you to be sick...for our, um, concert on Friday."

He cracks a grin. "So your concern is a selfish one, yeah?"

"No, of course not." I know he's joking, but I don't want him to think I don't care about him.

"Just kidding," he says quickly. "I think I'm just going to lie down. Shouldn't be wandering the girls' halls anyway. My tutorial is in an hour, and I don't want to upset Ms. Agailya."

"Does she ever get upset?"

"Not easily. Only when I'm caught in places I shouldn't be." He manages a smile as he turns to go. "See you tomorrow, maybe?"

I brighten. "Yeah. I hope so."

"Me too," he says, and trudges down the hallway.

At that moment, Wil appears at the top of the stairs. Ethan waves hello to him, and the two exchange awkward greetings. Wil watches Ethan trudge down the stairs and then, his hands in his pockets, strolls towards me.

"He looks rough," he says as he approaches Jia's door.

"I wasn't talking to him for long," I say, crossing my arms.

Wil raises his eyebrows. "Oookay. Wasn't accusing you of anything."

"Good."

Jia opens her door. Her gaze passes over me quickly, and it harbours no resentment from our conversation this morning. I feel relieved. "I thought I heard you guys out here."

"Ready?" Wil asks her.

"Yeah. Wait, here." She produces a bag of apples. "Just got these this morning from the grocery store. I've had one already, and I'm fine. Hungry?"

"Yes," I reply, holding out my hand.

Jia hands me an apple, which I bite into desperately. Wil takes one as well. Jia takes one more from the bag, then throws the rest on her bed and shuts and locks her door. The three of us devour the fruit like ravenous hyenas eating fresh kill while we head down the stairs.

It's not until we're outside, and I've eaten the apple down to the core, that I notice Misty hasn't joined us. Wil eats his core, and once we've made sure no one is around, Jia digs a hole in the grass with her foot and dumps her core in. She gestures for me to hand her mine, and I do. Of course—if the Collective got a hold of our DNA, even just our saliva, who knows what it could be used for? Not that they don't have it on file already. But I don't want them to have any more of me than they already have. Who knows what *Gattaca*-like protocols they have for collecting stray hairs and skin flakes escaping me every second? Surely the Collective doesn't waste time with separating dust from DNA—they're probably waiting until I'm "just right" to harvest to get everything. My apple core joins the others in the ground and Jia covers them up with dirt. It is better to be paranoid than foolish.

"Misty's not coming?" I ask, wiping apple bits off my face.

"No," Wil replies shortly, and trudges onward.

I frown at Jia until she explains. "She's locked herself in her room. We tried to get her to come earlier in the day, but when she resorted to screaming, well, some of the other girls told Ms. Agailya that Wil was in the girls' dorms, and, well, he sort of got in trouble."

"No wonder he's bitter, then. At least he had the courage to come back."

Jia smiles a bit at this, and together we follow Wil. "He said that you went to Ms. Agailya yesterday."

I can only assume that he picked this up with his mind. "I did, yeah."

"You talked about majors? Have you decided on your second one yet?"

I shake my head. "No. We didn't really"—I lower my voice—"didn't really talk much about that after all."

Jia's eyes widen. "Did she...did she agree to help us?"

It's my turn to be bitter. "No. She won't." I slide my gaze to hers. "You said you asked for her help before?"

She nods. "Yes. But in the end, it's not in her interest to help us."

"Why's that?"

"Because no matter how much she despises the Collective with her very being, she is still devoted to its cause," Wil says, spinning around. "You girls going to gossip all afternoon, or are we going to do this?"

I fold my arms. "No need to be rude. I was just curious."

His expression softens. "Sorry, Ingrid. Just...she gave me a rough time."

My stomach flutters as he stares at me for longer than I think is appropriate. I remind myself that I'm not the girl Wil likes. It's not that Wil is unattractive. Kinda nerdy? Definitely cute. But Wil reminds me too much of the older brother I never had, the way he can assume a leadership position.

Jia leads us to the applied sciences building. Unlike Conrod Building, which is Wil's engineering lab, this building is closer to the main dorms and doesn't look like a solid silver prison. It's more like the art building that Ethan toils away in on the other side of campus, and this thought puts me in a better mood. The golden plate above the door says *John Dewey Centre*.

"Laura's working on stuff but shouldn't be too busy to talk," Jia says as she swipes her key card across the black box next to the door. The double doors click open, and we venture inside. She lowers her voice to a whisper. "If Professor Perkins happens to be there, or come in, just say you're test subjects for Laura's experiment."

Wil stiffens. "Test subjects?"

"Don't worry, it's just cognitive psychology. Identifying patterns, choosing blue or red when a sound is played, that sort of thing." She smiles up at him. "You're not scared of a bit of pattern recognition, are you?"

"Choosing blue or red," I say. "I think we've all chosen red so far, yes?"

Wil wipes his glasses on his shirt and smiles at the

Matrix reference. "I just thought the research might be more…advanced."

"Well, it's not. Technically she'd prefer to do her tests on local school children, since that is her field, but, of course, the *school* won't let her."

We climb a set of stairs to the second floor, where Jia swipes her card at another set of doors. We follow her down a carpeted hallway of offices until she stops abruptly at a door labelled *Cognitive Psych Lab 204.* Newspaper comics have been cut out and taped to the entrance, all of them containing psychology-related jokes.

Jia takes a deep breath and then opens the door to the lab. It's not at all what I'm expecting. Instead of rows of tables and computers or other science equipment, there are three leather couches and a coffee table in the middle of the room. Two students are slumped on the couches, reading magazines. There are three doors on the opposite wall—more offices, judging by the name plates.

We cross the room and go through a half-open door. It's not so much an office as it is a cramped-closet computer lab. There's a desk that runs the length of the wall, which is sprinkled with outlets. The room is not much wider than my wingspan. We crowd in, and Jia shuts the door behind us.

We're not alone. A girl with shoulder-length frizzy brown hair looks up from her laptop. A smattering of freckles dots her otherwise blemish-free face. "Oh, hey, Jia."

"Hey, Laura," Jia replies, smiling awkwardly. "How's it going?"

"Ugh. Don't get me started about Professor Perkins. I told you what happened yesterday, right? He—"

Laura gets up and lowers her laptop screen, then suddenly seems to notice Wil and me. "Oh. Hey. Are you waiting for an experiment to start? 'Cause if you are—"

"No, we're friends of Jia's. I'm Ingrid."

Wil holds out his hand. "Wil."

Laura exchanges an *oh my god he's cute* look with Jia as she shakes Wil's hand. "Laura. Nice to meet you, *Wil.*"

"Same," Wil says as he gently pries his hand from her handshake, which goes on for longer than what's considered polite.

"Jia's been telling me all about you," she says, falling back into her seat and gazing up at him. "You're an engineering major?"

His steely gaze flickers to Jia, who looks as if she's going to be sick with embarrassment. "Yes," Wil says shortly.

Save me from this, Wil's voice booms in my head.

"Hey, are you going to that event that's going on in the cafeteria?" I say, trying to sound casual.

"You heard about that *too*?" Laura is whispering now. "A *protest*. Saw a bunch of signs for it. No one knows who put them up. I heard the professors are *pissed* though. Do you guys have anything to do with it?"

My throat tightens. "No, no. Do you?"

"No!" Her whisper is full of emotion and surprise. "I was hoping you'd know. People keep making guesses. I thought it was maybe some people in the political science department though, you know, doing an experiment or something. But…I don't know. Something really weird happened to me yesterday."

Jia looks worried. I start to panic. "Oh?"

"Yeah. Really weird. I went to print off instructions for my next experiment and only had five credits left on my card. I was pretty sure I had at least fifty. So I went and asked Madison to see if I could borrow her card, and that worked fine, but I guess Professor Perkins overheard me asking. And he pulled me into his office."

"Oh no!" Jia says, with just the right mix of concern and disinterest.

"Yeah! So Professor Perkins pulled me into his office and started asking me all these questions. It was *so weird*. Asked me if I'd used my card recently, and of course I said yes because I use it all the time. I had like five hundred credits at the beginning of the semester because I use it so much. I don't know, he wouldn't tell me why he was asking all these questions. It was just really awkward."

My face flushes. I just want this conversation to be over.

"And I heard a rumour this morning that a bunch of people who use their photocopying credits a lot were called into different professors' offices and questioned. And seeing all the posters up everywhere... I'm not sure, but whoever is running this protest, seems like they found a way to steal our codes." Laura's eyes are wide with conspiracy. "You guys should check your credits."

I wanted to leave some credits on her account, Wil explains telepathically. *So I pulled some random accounts and used some credits from them. I thought it might look less suspicious. Maybe I was wrong.*

"Yeah, I'll do that," Jia says, glancing back and forth between the two of us. "So you think you're going to go?"

"Are you going to go?" Laura is looking at Wil.

Wil struggles not to look uncomfortable with the attention. "Yeah, I'll check it out."

"Oh! Well then, I might check it out too," she replies, grinning.

"Ookay," Jia says. The look on Jia's face verges on furious at her friend's attempt to tread on what Jia considers her territory.

I interrupt her before she prematurely ushers us out of the room. "So, Wil, maybe you can save her a spot? I hear the cafeteria might be really crowded."

"Really? You think that many people are going?" Laura asks, her eyes wide.

I shrug. "I heard some girls talking about it in the hallway in my dorm. They seemed to think a bunch of their friends were going."

"The cafeteria is not going to run out of space," Jia remarks.

"No, but what if they stop letting people in? Like the professors, they could put a stop to it if they thought something bad was going down," Laura says. She chews on her nails. "Wil, maybe you should meet me like a half hour before, and we could go together?"

"We'll all meet a half hour before," Jia says, throwing me a cold look.

"Yeah, sure," Laura says dismissively. "I want to be the first one there. There's a bunch of stuff that's super weird at the school. I hope there's an open mic session. I'd totally get up there and talk about my experiences."

I purse my lips. Jia was right. Laura is eager to speak out against Sparkstone University. This will make her one of the Collective's prime targets for sure.

"Yeah, you should do that," Wil says encouragingly.

"I will! Oh, I'm so glad you guys are going. It's nice to not be alone in this kind of stuff, you know?"

"I know," I say quietly.

"Hey Ingrid, don't you have that thing in fifteen minutes?" Jia asks me, raising an eyebrow.

That thing. "Oh…yeah," I say slowly. "I guess we'd better go."

"Oh." Laura looks disappointed. "Yeah, I guess I'd better finish my stuff. Nice to meet you guys, though."

"Same," Wil and I say at the same time, and Laura beams at Wil's voice.

"See you tomorrow," Jia says icily to her friend, and quickly ushers us out of the room and the lab.

"That was relatively painless," I say once we're back in the hallway.

Jia is silent and gives me the cold shoulder. "We're set for tomorrow, then?" she asks Wil.

I've analyzed the sample. I should be able to feed the information through Laura if she gets up to speak. Otherwise, I might just spread it through everyone's minds, try to get them angry enough to act, Wil says telepathically.

"You mean…you want to incite a riot? You can do that?" I whisper.

Wil looks somewhat unsure. "I think I can."

"That means you're not coming to the library with us," Jia says.

He shakes his head and starts off down the hallway. "You don't need me. Tomorrow before the protest I'll modify your bracelets to do all the work I would."

"But…but once the professors find out there's a riot in the cafeteria, you could be caught. They might…harvest you." Jia's voice wavers.

"I'll be careful," he says with a grim smile. He glances back at me. "Just make sure you get that treatise."

I nod solemnly. "It's there. I know it is. I saw it."

"Good," he says. "'Cause if this fails, we're in a lot of trouble. And if it succeeds"—he shoves his hands in his pockets—"we might just be one step closer to pushing the Collective out of Sparkstone."

CHAPTER 8

We're standing outside Rogers Hall forty-five minutes before the protest is scheduled to start, but already there are people filing in. That could be because it's supper time, though. We had to schedule it during cafeteria hours so that we wouldn't be breaking into the place, and because that's when people would come anyway. If Wil's theory is correct, no one will be under the influence of Gen-Grow tonight—everyone will be lucid, not in a dream-like stupor from the food. He touches our bracelets one by one and programs them so we can get past potential security in the underground library.

You'll stay for the first ten minutes, Wil says telepathically. *Then, get out of here. Scout the library. I will join you, once there's enough ruckus here, and once Laura is safe. Use the bracelets only when you have to. If the aliens discover too many missing moments on the cameras, they'll know what we're up to and come after us. Once you get out of the library, text my cell. Something in code, like, "Where are you?"*

"That sounds like a question we'd ask anyway," I say.

"That's the point," Misty says with a sneer. There are deep, dark circles around her eyes, and it's not her makeup today. She must have lost a lot of sleep last night. I hope she doesn't flake out on us tonight. This heist has to work.

A few minutes later, Laura shows up. A few other students trail behind her and Jia greets all of them. Laura gushes at Wil, Jia struggles to maintain her distaste, but he is civil towards both of them.

We allow the woman in front of the cafeteria to scan our key cards. I expect her to give us a lecture for not showing up at the cafeteria more often—that's what happened to me the first day I came, and I'd only missed one meal—but she simply smiles and waves us through. This makes me nervous. The Collective isn't putting a stop to this protest. They know it's happening. Maybe they're going to let it happen. Maybe they believe it will fail.

We take our places in the cafeteria. I sit in the middle of the room next to girls I don't know. People are chatting, sitting around at tables, eating, but no one is actively engaged or interested in protesting. Most are finishing their meals. Tonight, the stage and the piano upon it send flutters of fear through me. Someone has set up a microphone. Laura is at the foot of the stage with Jia, but she looks unsure about the ordeal, now that we have around five hundred students gathered in one place. Wil sits at a nearby table, hands neatly folded, eyes closed, probably concentrating on the whereabouts of the professors to make sure we won't be prematurely interrupted. He needs to get Laura to speak soon, or we will lose this crowd.

Misty is by the door, playing on her phone. I hope that in her boredom she's poised to strike, should the Collective rear its ugly alien head. If it does, she promised to set some fires in nearby trash cans as a distraction. Unfortunately she does nothing to stop the group of students leaving the cafeteria.

I see no sign of Ethan. He'd said he'd be here, maybe. Though he's probably off doing an art project, or hanging out with Kimberly, or . . . or just avoiding a lame-ass protest attempt. I run a hand through my tangled hair.

A girl next to me shrugs and stands up. "Isn't there supposed to be a protest happening? It's pretty lame."

"Must have been a joke," says another girl beside her.

"No, wait," I say. "Something's going to happen really soon, I promise."

"Oh?" The first girl looks confused, and intrigued. "Are you one of the organizers?"

"Um, well no, but . . . "

My gaze passes over the stage again, and the grand piano at the front. It's alone, and its top is closed. The light streaming in from the window highlights it in a heavenly glow. Dust has settled over its top. It hasn't been touched in a while.

Something in me shudders. A lance of goosebumps strikes deep into my core, and in that moment, it's as if I'm in a dream. The faint buzz of the room quiets.

There's nothing left for you here, the voice of doubt whispers. *Your family is in jeopardy. You don't have superpowers, none that you can control anyway. This protest is a failure. The Collective will come and take your life, smash it to bits just like it smashed your harp. And what will you have to show for it? When Ethan is an old man, he will look back on life, and if his memory is able, he will say, "Whatever happened to that girl with the red hair, the musician at that Canadian university? What did she ever do that mattered?"*

The noise of the cafeteria returns. The girl is still waiting for me to respond.

And so I do the only thing I can do.

I'm walking towards the stage, but I feel as if my legs are carrying me there, as if I'm moving through clouds and my appendages are wispy bursts of fluff that will dissipate into nothing with a whisper. I'm pushed forward by a gentle breeze behind me, and at the same time, I'm pulled by the grand piano. Its dark, shiny skin is calling me. The keys, they want my touch.

Time has moved forward. I'm in front of the piano. I haven't yet disturbed the other songs playing in the room—the frantic, confused, mud-brown tones of a million conversations glued together, a thousand painted stories overlapping on one canvas because there's just not enough room for everyone to have a separate space.

The weight on my hands is so heavy, so very heavy.

Play, something within me says.

I will disturb the silence. I will make my mark.

The instant my fingers press down on the keys, something within me shifts. I know, from this moment forward, there's no going back. I really cannot turn around and tell my former self to not step onto this stage and not disturb the silence. I am creating a new self with each note I play. I'm creating a melody of former selves, a red-blue double helix that twists around the room. I don't look up from the keys. But I can feel the eyes of my peers. Everyone has quieted. They're all paying attention to me now.

The song doesn't resemble anything I know, not at first.

It's something new I'm making up as I go. And yet, it feels as familiar to me as ... as Joseph G. Campbell does.

That's when I realize: *I'm playing* his *song.*

The music flows from somewhere ethereal, through me, into the piano keys and out into the world and into my ears and the ears of everyone in the room. Every new note not only describes me in present time, but also calls to Joseph G. Campbell, wherever he is, somewhere in the depths of my mind but also somewhere else that is timeless.

I look over at the students, who have gathered at the foot of the stage. And there he is. Weaving his way through the crowd of students. Shimmering. Handsome. Present, in a way that he was not on the mother ship, and in Sunni's journal. The students keep their distance from him, as if they can sense his presence.

I knew you would call me, he says with his mind, the way Wil silently communicates but somehow deeper. His voice vibrates inside my chest. *You speak the sweet-sounding language of home.*

The music is the key, I realize. His song drew him to me. Through these notes, we are connected. I'm not sure if anyone else can see him. But that's when I know for certain that he is real, that I did not somehow birth him, that I am not crazy.

The other man of my heart also approaches the stage. Unlike Campbell, he does not stop before the edge of the platform. No, he climbs the steps in time with my dark forest-green melodies. Ethan's guitar is slung over his back, and he swings it around like a rock star and joins in flawlessly. Part of me, some small forgotten part that cares about earthly things, is worried that we'll go in different directions with the song. But he's following my lead, watching my fingers dance over the keys. And I'm watching him. He plays with a confidence I don't feel, as though he's stood on stage in front of thousands of adoring fans before. Like he was born to perform. Ethan's strand of sound mixes with mine in a way that makes my body ache. This moment belongs to us.

The cafeteria door bursts wide open and Jadore and a team of four security guards march in. I falter for just a moment, playing an E instead of an F-sharp chord. Under those dark sunglasses I know she's surveying the crowd, and her lips curl into a snarl.

I'm in trouble. Bigger trouble than I've been in before.

Ethan covers my floundering. I don't dare stop. Joseph G. Campbell is at the edge of the stage, lifting an adoring hand towards me. Like he's asking me to come with him to some place I don't know. I don't take my eyes off him as the song continues to swell and pour from me.

The crowd parts and in my periphery, Jadore marches towards my mysterious alien protector. And that's when I realize: she can see him. She taps her cane, mismatching the beats and refusing to keep time with the tune, and then holds it up to eye level. She's going to attack him. She's going to do something horrible, I just know it.

So I do the only thing I can.

I stop playing.

Joseph G. Campbell blinks out of existence just as Jadore swings her cane wildly. Instead of hitting the invisible alien, the cane smashes into three students and knocks them over into the people behind them. Shouts of "What the hell?" and "Professor, do you need help?" are drowned out by the clapping and cheering from my peers.

145

"Encore! Encore!" some students chant, the ones in the back who can't see the disturbance Jadore has created. Ethan strums a few chords, as if feeling out my willingness to play another song, but I swing my legs around the piano stool.

Jadore's anger emanates in waves, but almost everyone is still too enraptured by our performance to pay her any mind. She stands defiant, silent amidst the dying noise, and stares death at me beneath those shades. She's preparing to swing again.

"Hi, Professor. Come for the show?" Ethan asks into the microphone while fingering a complicated string of notes.

She growls at him, low and inhuman. But she wouldn't dare expose herself here. The students at the front look to me for an explanation of Jadore's behaviour.

Get off the stage, Wil warns me. *The—*

A stout man with a balding head struts into the gymnasium. In his left hand, he clutches a megaphone. He too is flanked by hafelglob in human form—their quivering nostrils, awkward strides, and empty stares give them away immediately. Ms. Agailya trails him by several paces, her long fingers worrying her skirt. She gives me an apologetic, wary look and then returns her gaze to the stout man. The students exchange whispers as he makes his way to Jadore.

The president and vice-chancellor of Sparkstone University, Wil says to me.

I raise my eyebrows.

Wil answers my unspoken question. *He's human, we think. But the Collective's hold on him is tight.*

I wouldn't think it to look at him. His fury hits me in waves as he crosses the room towards Laura and the group of protesters. A few of the people in the back cease their chanting of "encore!"

"What is going on here?" the president demands through his megaphone. "This is an unauthorized gathering. All large-scale oppositions to campus regulations *must* have the proper permits to stage a protest. Who is responsible for throwing this absurd rally? Is this part of some sort of project?" His gaze flies to me. "Explain yourself."

My stomach is laden with dread. Ethan and I exchange glances. I draw in a breath, preparing to take the fall, as Laura weaves her way through the crowd and runs on stage. Ethan steps aside as she grabs the microphone from its stand.

"Thank you, Ingrid, for that. President Dean. I'm glad you could come." Her tone verges on saucy. "We're *protesting*."

Part of the crowd, infused with confidence from our music, cheers Laura on with a round of applause. Oh god. It's working. This protest is *happening*.

Laura shakes her fist in the air and speaks to her peers. "What do we want?"

There's an awkward pause. The posters did say the protest was against the food, but that seems to have been forgotten. Opposing the Collective's control is the real fight here.

Then I hear Jia's voice from the middle of the crowd. She is invisible, but her voice is loud and clear. "The food is poison! We want better food!"

"Poison?" Laura mutters, but then I see a flash of ideas in Laura's eye—Wil is filling her head with information. "Yes! The food is poison! Packed with chemicals! Nothing here is organic. Do you know what's really in the food? The professors want us to be filled with harmful chemicals!"

That's a start. Some of the girls in the crowd light up with fury and throw their fists in the air. "Chemicals in the food? What chemicals?"

Perhaps by Jia's doing, a chant ripples from the middle of the crowd. "Better food! Better food!"

Laura's quick as a whip. "Yes! And when do we want it?"

"Enough!"

President Dean holds up his megaphone, and his voice effectively drowns out the chanting. There's another round of "what do we want," but it's wasted. The president belts out his commands loud and clear, with Jadore's spindly fingers wrapped around his forearm.

"You," he says, pointing an accusatory finger at Laura. "Come with me."

I shoot a glance at Wil. He's deep in concentration. I take a deep breath. I have to trust that Wil can keep Laura under control. More innocent people will not be murdered, not if I can help it. Not after I was so close to getting Joseph G. Campbell to my side.

Laura's face pales, and there's a brief blip of vacancy in her eyes before she responds with Wil's implanted words. "No, President Dean. I am going nowhere." She raises her hands to rally the students. "Together, we are strong. Everyone! What do we want?"

"Better food!" I shout.

Others chant with me, but I had forgotten about my place on stage, and the volume of my voice betrays me. Jadore's gaze hones in on my exposed form.

"That's enough," the president booms through his megaphone. "If you leave now, you will not be punished.

But if you stay, you will face the consequences: your projects, which I'm sure you've all worked hard on, will no longer count as credit towards your degree."

Silence descends. Then, as if by mass mental agreement, students trickle out of the cafeteria. Laura pleads, but her cries are lost over the worried stampede vying for the exit. I see Wil struggling for control of not only Laura, but everyone in the room. His head falls into his hands—it's too much. It's too late for Misty to create a distraction. Even Ethan shoots me a look, asking if I'm leaving or staying. When I don't move, his gaze becomes apologetic.

The project ultimatum doesn't matter to me. Jadore will not let me give up my project about Joseph G. Campbell for anything. But Wil, and Jia? Even Misty's project had some importance to her. I see them slowly capitulating, joining the crowd to leave, but the stampede has slowed to a snail's pace with the sheer number of bodies looking to escape.

Jadore's gaze is clear. I will not be losing my project privileges like the other dissenters. I have something much more valuable in the balance. My father's life. Her grin is pure evil. This is what she was waiting for. This is the excuse she needs to kill my father and tighten her grip on me.

We are doomed.

I will be here at Sparkstone for good.

I will never see my family again.

PART TWO

Go bravely into that darkness, so that you may shine your own light.

—J.G.C., *Campbell's Multiple Verses*

CHAPTER 9

Someone grabs me from behind, and I struggle. It's Ohz. He must have slipped onto the stage in the commotion. His grip is unmerciful as he rests his whiskery chin on my shoulder and yanks my arm hard behind my back.

"Crosskey has done a bad thing," he hisses in my ear, his breath uncomfortably warm. "Tried to warn Crosskey, Ohz did. Crosskey not listen. Crosskey disobey. Cause trouble. Mistress kill your father, now."

My gaze never leaves Jadore as Ohz drags me from the stage because she's my true captor. All around me, maintenance workers and other people wearing security uniforms are grabbing my fellow students and roughly escorting them out of the cafeteria. I strain my neck, looking desperately to see where Ethan has gone, but there is no sign of him.

"No permit, no protest," President Dean is shouting, over and over again, hands waving. "Campus freedom privileges revoked."

Jadore points at me, Laura, and my friends, who are

scattered in the crowd, and whispers something in the president's ear. He turns a hawk's eye on us, finding us each in turn in the crowd with uncanny speed.

"Confined to quarters," says President Dean, pointing like a judge laying down our fate with an invisible gavel.

Could be worse, Wil says as two security guards flank him and wrap their hands around his muscled forearms. He does not resist as they push him through the throng of students and out of sight.

But I know it's worse. Jadore is not just confining me to quarters. Something terrible is going to happen to my family. She'll never buy that Laura or any other non-Spark is behind this. I'm in the crowd, and so it's my fault, and my friends' fault, and everything I know and love will suffer for it.

Ohz licks my earlobe before releasing me. "Will leave Crosskey now for punishment."

I shudder and wipe his salvia from my ear. Security guards close their long, spindly hands around my arms as I tense and grit my teeth. I will not show Jadore that I am weak. I will not let her take my dignity.

I conjure thoughts of home. My mum, and my dad. My music. I try to recall Joseph G. Campbell's tune. Pieces of it return, though whatever force fuelled it does not return. It is better than nothing. Jadore cannot read thoughts, I'm fairly certain, but I know she sees my resolve. She holds up her cane, level with my neck, and prevents the guards from taking me further.

"Leave us," she says to the guards. "I will handle this one. Assist the others."

The security guards don't question her authority. I feel the absence of their hands immediately as they release me and run to assist Misty's guards. A string of swear words in at least three languages explodes from Misty's mouth. She hisses at them like a stray cat as they surround her, steering her where they want her to go. I catch a glint of fire in one of her palms. The guards are part of the Collective, and they know that touching her is inviting death.

"This way," Jadore commands.

I draw in a deep breath and hold my head high as I follow her, taking long strides to keep up. I am almost lost in the crowd at one point, but she grabs the scruff of my shirt and pulls me through the crowd, out of the cafeteria, up the stairs, and out of the building. Then she releases me and continues across the path towards my dorm. I could try to run, but I fear for my parents' safety. I struggle to keep pace with the alien professor.

"You were warned," she says. She's not even pretending to let her cane lead the way. "This charade was a waste of time."

The grass invades my sandals and presses between my toes. I remain silent.

"I know it was you and your little friend group that organized this. Using that girl as your mouthpiece? Don't think we didn't notice your pathetic attempts to cover your tracks." She tosses the cane to her left hand, and it bobs forward and back as we walk. The blade could slip out of the top and slice me to pieces in moments. Perhaps that is her plan for when we are alone.

"And it's extremely convenient that our last shipment was contaminated. Inconvenient for me, but not a terrible inconvenience. I had another batch flown in."

I push through the door to Rita House, but Jadore keeps

up. The lobby is eerily empty, and I count the seconds until my demise. I start for the stairs, and Jadore's nails dig into my arm.

"You play the martyr well," she says. "But the concept is wasted on me. There are many things of yours that I can still take. Did you know that your mother phoned here yesterday with an update on your father? She couldn't get through on your cell phone, which is a shame. The tower must have been under maintenance." Her dark lips brush against my ear, sending harsh chills down my body. "He is stable for now. If he wakes up, it will be a miracle if he ever walks again. Of course, he could worsen, and spiral downward, if given the right...push." She shoves me towards the stairs and holds her cane against the small of my back. "Up you go, little Crosskey. I am still behind you."

The lump in my throat is strong, and I hold my breath as I climb the stairs. So that's why I haven't heard from my parents. It feels as if Jadore is choking the life out of me. I imagine falling on the stairs now, and Jadore ripping me in two and devouring whatever part of me it is that she needs to further her agenda.

I make it to the third floor without dying. Only one girl passes us in the hallway, and she averts her gaze as soon as she sees Jadore. I slip my key card from my pocket and unlock the door. Jadore enters my room. There is no question that she intends to continue my torture in the one semi-private space I call my own. I try not to think about Sunni's journal, hidden in the bathroom.

"This will be your prison for the next twenty-four hours, until I convene the council and decide what your fate will be," Jadore says. "Your key card will no longer work. Attempt to escape, and your father will be killed. Attempt to contact your friends, and your father will be killed. Sometime tomorrow, someone will come get you, and the Collective will lay down your fate." Her smile is cruel. "Do you have anything to say to me at this time, or will your pathetic silence be it?"

I look up at her, and then down at the remains of my keyboard, its detached keys stacked in fives across the exposed matrix circuit—the fragile electronic innards of the instrument. "What will happen when I die?"

The surprise on her shaded face is quickly masked by determination. "You will be assessed by our DNA specialists. Dissected, most likely. They will study your internal organs and determine what will be broken down for use within the Collective. In your case...because the council has determined that your DNA is vital to our primary objective, we will attempt to consult with our investors to see if there is enough of you to achieve our goal. If not, we will attempt to synthesize more, if economically and scientifically feasible. If it is determined that there is not enough, then—"

"Stop it." I bunch my fingers into fists. "Stop talking about me like I'm not a person."

Jadore snorts. "Wherever did you get the idea that you are a person?"

I don't turn to face her as she leaves, and I don't check the door, because the loud click makes it clear that I'm trapped here. The camera above my bed weighs on my shoulders with its red light and all-seeing eye. I am paralyzed by my fear of death, and by my fear of obscurity. Twenty-four hours and it will be as if I never existed.

No. I can't let my last day on Earth be like this. I have to show them that I am a person. I have to reclaim this time as my own.

I am not religious. I don't know if there is an afterlife that awaits me, or if this afterlife is fashioned according to my behaviour in the here and now. But I kneel before my broken keyboard, hands clasped, head tipped to the ceiling. If this is the last evening I have on this planet, then I will make it count.

I can't give up hope. It is not the only thing I have left, I remind myself. The Collective can take away my friends, they can deny me the right to talk to my parents. They have my future coiled around their fingers, tighter than twisted double helices. But there is one thing they can't take away from me.

My instruments are destroyed, but that doesn't mean that my music cannot be released. My voice slices the silence in a long, vibrating A and fills the room with the rich tones of tomatoes and cherries. One second, two seconds, three seconds I hold the note. The A chord is red—the first primary colour from which all else is born. Red is the sound of defiance, and I make sure the room is brimming with it so that I can bathe in my own sense of justice.

You can take my life, I tell the cameras and whoever is listening. *But you cannot take my song.*

I wake up sometime later, my head slumped against the broken keyboard. My neck is sore from the angle. My brain lulls me into another half sleep before I will myself to stand—one hand grasping a bundle of broken keys, the other gripping the blankets on my bed. I check my alarm clock. Almost eleven-thirty. The darkness outside confirms that it is time for the good little students at Sparkstone to hop in their beds and get their well-deserved sleep to prepare for another day of gruelling research and development before their time comes to be harvested.

The bed calls to me, but sleeping seems like a waste of time. Instead I go to the bathroom, splash some water on my face, and brush my hair. So much for breaking into the underground library tonight. Or ever. I'm contemplating a shower and delving into Sunni's journal for answers when I hear a knock on the door.

The knock is non-intrusive; polite, almost. Could it be Jia, invisible, come to rescue me? I saunter to the door as the potential visitor raps once more, and I peek through the peephole.

I exhale his name. "Ethan."

"Oh good, you're still awake," he replies. "Can you let me in?"

"I wish I could, but I'm locked in."

"Okay, this is worth a try. I'll just..." He pulls a key card from his pocket and swipes it by the sensor. To my surprise, it beeps, and the door clicks. I stand back as he opens the door, and there he is, inches from me. My rescuer. My hero. Though his nose is somewhat red, and his cheeks rosy, he looks a lot better than he did yesterday.

"Ethan." I say his name again because I love the way it tastes in my mouth. "How did you...?"

"Ms. Agailya said that you got confined to quarters. But I uh...managed to...shall we say *acquire* a master key card from her office. Don't think she saw me slip it into my pocket." His smirk fades. "Hope you don't think ill of me for—"

"No." I could kiss him again. It would really be a goodbye kiss this time. "So you had a meeting with Ms. Agailya this late?"

"A couple of hours ago, yeah. I missed tutorial today so I had to make up for it with a private meeting. She also had some stern words to say to me about what we did at the protest."

"The song," I say breathlessly. "It was beautiful. Thank you for...for playing with me."

"Yeah, of course." He smiles casually.

I can't think of anything else to say. "I...I can't believe you came for me."

"Can't let my girl rot in here while the night is young," he replies with a wink. I melt on the inside—*my girl?* Does that mean what I think it means? His gaze drifts around the room. "Not that your room isn't nice or anything." He frowns when he sees the keyboard. "What happened here?"

My stomach twists with embarrassment. "Someone broke into my room and destroyed it."

Ethan swears under his breath. "Bloody hell, Ingrid. That's not right. Did you tell Ms. Agailya or one of the other professors? Maybe they'd replace it for you?"

I shake my head. "I'm not sure if they would."

He looks at me with a renewed resolve. "That's it. I know what we're going to do."

"You do?"

"Yes." His smile is back. He holds out a hand. "Come with me."

"Where am I going?" I ask hesitantly. Jadore has

threatened the lives of my family and my friends and has placed a timer on my life. I feel as though I have the right to refuse any activity that will waste my precious minutes, regardless of who wishes my company.

"Trust me." He brushes my cheek. "You do, don't you?"

"I do." The words leave me quickly because they are true.

"Then c'mon." Holding up the master key card like a Monopoly Get Out of Jail Free card, he gestures to the dorm door. "The night is ours."

I hesitate. My eyes flit to the camera above my bed. They will know I'm gone. It may be seconds, or minutes if we're lucky, before they catch up with us and escort me back to my room. My father—what if they kill my father because I set foot outside of this room?

Then again, Ethan made it all the way here without problems. We've been chatting for at least five minutes. Plenty of time for Jadore to set her guards on me. Perhaps this is a test.

"Something wrong?" Ethan asks.

"I'm...I'm really not supposed to leave," I say reluctantly. "But...maybe half an hour with you will be all right. And if Jadore or someone catches us, I will submit to whatever punishment she sees fit. No one else, just me. I will take the responsibility." I say this for the camera's sake. *Consider this my last request,* I mouth to the red light. *Let me have this one joy.*

"Uh, sure," Ethan says. "But Ms. Agailya said that Jadore's off campus for the night. Gone home. So, I highly doubt she'll catch us."

This lightens my heart. I wonder briefly if she lives on the mother ship, or if she's in one of the cookie-cutter

160

houses. I slip into a pair of old flip-flops and then Ethan and I step into the corridor. Just because Jadore isn't on campus doesn't mean she doesn't have access to the cameras. I have to be careful not to let my infatuation with Ethan sweep me into dangerous waters. Not that I'm not in dangerous waters already.

Ethan smiles at me. "You're not afraid of sneaking out, are you?"

"I am, a little."

"I am too, a little." He swipes the master key card across the pad beside my door, and the light blinks red. I think about calling out to Wil, to see if he can hear me, to see if he can rig the camera feed in my room, but then Ethan grabs my hand and pulls me down the hallway. His touch distracts me from all further thought. We are not just sneaking out of a dorm room. We are going on a magical adventure.

Upon reaching the stairs, Ethan puts a finger to his mouth and tightens his grip on my hand. There's a twinkle in his eye. "There might be a security guard at the desk."

"What about the cameras?" I whisper, flicking my gaze to above the door we just came through.

"Cameras...?" He follows my gaze. "Is that what those are? I always suspected...but really? Cameras?"

"They're all over campus. Let's hurry outside. I don't think they have many eyes out there."

"Ingrid Stanley," he says huskily. "You aren't scared at all, are you?"

"I am," I say. *And you'd be scared too if you knew the risk I was taking right now.*

We sneak out of Rita House with little difficulty. The security guard at the desk is sleeping. He looks human, but I can't be sure. I'm too excited by Ethan's grip to really take a closer look.

Once outside, under the blanket of night, I ask, "So, where are we going?"

"Just don't let go of me. I don't want to lose you out here."

I squeeze his hand to reassure him that I am not going anywhere, and together we take off across the grass. It must have rained while I was asleep because the greenery is wet between my toes. Though it's cold and my feet want to find solid ground as fast as possible, I relish the moment: my quickening heart, the smell of the air in its post-rain state, the faint lamps that sprinkle the campus walkways, the twinkle of the lights as one by one they blink out and Sparkstone workers lay down their heads to sleep.

Ethan leads me to a small building with just one window, on the right side. Unlike the other buildings at Sparkstone, this one is little more than a trailer. Once again he swipes his master key card and the door admits us.

Inside the closet-sized entryway, there are three doors. Ethan gestures to the door at my right while I inspect the ceiling for red lights and other signs of surveillance. Nothing, as far as I can see. There's a keypad in front of the door Ethan wants to access. He swipes the card again, and the keypad flashes green.

"You ready for my surprise?" he asks, grinning like a child at Christmas.

"Yeah," I say, nodding, my excitement swelling and matching his.

He swings the door open and leads me inside. I gasp. It's a music room. I should have known that Sparkstone had one. They have almost everything else. Four keyboards are set up against the far wall, as well as one grand piano, and there are a variety of other instruments—guitars, a few violins propped up on stands, and even Irish pipes. I ache to hear the music of my ancestors, to hear the songs I know all too well sung by familiar voices. It is the music that makes me forget about my responsibilities.

It is the music that brought Joseph G. Campbell to me.

And maybe I'm too caught up in the moment, but I see no tell-tale red lights, or reflective glass, or round black holes. The Collective has not penetrated this room.

Ethan plops down on the bench in front of the grand piano. "Well? What do you think?"

"This is . . ." I twirl around, revelling in the atmosphere of the room. "This is beautiful. It's perfect." Ethan has given me a gift, and I don't know how to repay him.

"Thought you'd like it." His fingers splay over the keys, and as he applies his gentle touch, an A chord echoes through the room. "No harps in here, though. Sorry."

"That's all right. I'll sit next to you." I slide towards him on the piano bench. "I didn't know you played piano."

"It's not my main instrument. I only know a couple of chords, a few songs."

"Like what?" I position my hands on the upper octaves. "Anything we can play together?"

"You asking if I can play 'Chopsticks'?" He begins the jaunty tune and my hands fall instantly into position to play the higher octave. He smirks and shakes his head. "I know you can do better than that."

"Me? I was trying to cater to you."

"All right, all right." 'Chopsticks' becomes a slower melody in D major. "Do you recognize this tune?"

I shake my head and tentatively play the higher octave,

Clare C. Marshall

trying to predict the melody as Ethan creates it with his fingers.

"That's good," he says finally, rounding it out with a low G note. "Because I just wrote that, right now."

I gape and shove my shoulder into his playfully. "You don't just *dabble* with the piano," I say teasingly. "You're amazing."

"You're brilliant yourself."

"Do you have a name for it yet?"

"No, I just made it up now."

"Still. Something must have sparked it."

He gives me a sly look. "What do you think?"

My cheeks heat, and I refuse to make any assumptions. "Call it, 'Late Night Music Room Fun'?"

He laughs. "I know we can do better than that pathetic title."

But he doesn't suggest another and starts playing again. The song takes on an aimless but jaunty slant in G major. My hand ventures down the scale so I can input G minor— one of my favourite keys because it has a dark chocolate colour rimmed with an edge of energy that just makes you want to dance and go crazy. The major and minor pairing gives the tune the right amount of dark and light browns to make it feel homey.

I wind the tune to a close but Ethan is still playing. He brings it around to A minor—dark red—and then back to G before delving into E minor—a rich forest green. The song is in two-four time, but he's playing it like a slow air, and it fills the room with the haunted sounds of an enchanted realm. My hands rest in my lap and my eyes are closed as he paints me a story with his music.

"Ingrid."

My name is a splash of red and dark purple against the green. "Yeah?"

I open my eyes. He's staring intensely at the keys with a puzzled expression on his face. "I told you that sometimes I can't remember things...right?"

"Yes. But you don't have any memory problems, do you?"

"Well." He frowns. "I do. I've been having...sessions with the school psychiatrist. To help me remember. Sometimes I wake up and there are gaps—big black holes—in my memory. I don't think I'm forgetting important things...but I'm just afraid I'll wake up one day an old man and not remember anything about my life. Or anyone."

"Do you know what might be causing it?" I consider telling him not to eat the food in the cafeteria, that the Collective might be responsible for his memory loss.

"I..." His long fingers splay over the keys once more. "I'm afraid I've done something terrible. Something so awful that my brain is blocking it out. And now it's blocking out other things too."

"That..." I pause. It doesn't sound implausible. If Ethan went through something traumatic, it's possible that his mind is blocking it out. But having a blockage that spreads throughout the rest of his memories? That sounds...alien.

"Maybe you didn't do anything," I suggest. "Maybe something was done to you, and you don't want to remember it."

"Yeah, maybe." He doesn't sound convinced. "I just...I just have this feeling inside me that I've made a horrible mistake. But I don't remember what, or when I did it. And it drives me—!" He presses both his palms on the keys, emitting a deep mess of chords that strike blacks and browns and seas of sorrow within me.

"Sorry," he says, like he can feel what the music does to my body.

I rest my head on his shoulder. "I wish I could help you remember."

"Mmm." He's playing something again, a random compilation of notes. "Me too."

Our legs are touching. More than touching. We're pressing against each other. I want to melt into him. My fingers rest on the keys, and he creeps up the scale and lays a hand over mine as he plays the notes he needs.

I look at his face. He catches my gaze and the music fades—either because he's stopped playing, or because my vision is so overwhelmed with everything about him that my ears forget to hear.

He leans in. My breath catches. We're going to kiss again. His aftershave draws me in, and my nose brushes his. I'm breathing his air. He cups my cheek and shivers shoot down my spine. I want him. Oh God, I want him now.

Then, a jab of realization: I've been gone way too long. And no one has come after me. Either we have gotten away with sneaking out, or...

Or my father is dead.

Just as his lips graze mine, I shy away, shaking my head.

Ethan can't hide his surprise. "Ingrid? I'm sorry, did I...?"

"No," I whisper. "It's not...it's not you. I'm..." I'm so stupid, I should've just let him kiss me. I should've let myself have that one moment where the Collective wasn't dictating my fate. But the moment has passed. And I might be able to teleport myself in moments of great stress, but I can't travel back in time.

He shifts his leg away from mine and lays his fingers over the keys again to fill the air with something other than our awkwardness. "No, I just... assumed..."

There's so much in that word: *assumed. Yes,* I want to cry, *I do like you, I do want to kiss you, I do want to be with you. I risked everything to come here tonight to be with you and I failed to seize the night.*

"I should go back now," I say instead, because I'm afraid he will say it.

He nods. "I'll let you back into your room."

Please, stop me, hold me and tell me that I made a mistake. But that's a silly, girlish thought, fuelled by hormones and not by reason. He slides off the bench, and I touch where he once sat, feeling the warmth of his absence.

He faces the door, hands in his pockets, examining the three other keyboards. I stand and brush off my skirt. I don't want to leave it this way.

"Ethan. I want this," I say. It sounds strong and fierce in my head, but it comes out as barely a whisper. Fear chokes my words.

His gaze flits to mine. "I moved too fast, didn't I?"

"No, no, I'm... just afraid of being caught. In here. Right now."

Smirking, he pulls the key card from his pocket and plays with it. "There are no cameras in here."

"I know, but..."

"But what? C'mon, you're not one of those girls who flashes a smile and gives us a tease, all look, no... no touch?"

"What?" My face is burning now. "I'm *not* a—all look, no touch? What does that even mean?"

Now he looks more embarrassed than I do. "No, that came out wrong. I didn't mean it like that. I meant, if there's something here, something *real*"—he points at the ground—"then I don't want to play games. You kissed me first. You obviously had a reason for doing that."

I bury my face in my hands. This conversation is going all wrong. "I don't want to play games either. But I also don't appreciate being called a tease. I have *real...*" I'm choking again. "I just wish it didn't have to happen like this. I wish..."

"I brought you here because I thought you would like the room. The music," he says. His voice is gentler, but it's still lined with a hard edge. "What do you wish, Ingrid? I can't read your mind. Can I kiss you, or no?" His voice drops to a low whisper that I barely catch. "'Cause bloody hell, you drive me insane."

I step closer to him. "I don't mean to drive you insane. I'm not doing it on purpose. I'm not a *thing* you can ogle."

"I know that." He shakes his head. "Screw it."

And just when I think he's going to sweep me into his arms and kiss me passionately, he turns and pulls opens the door. He gestures. "After you, then."

I blew it. I totally blew it with Ethan. I grit my teeth and beat myself up on the inside as I pass by him and out into the entryway.

He pushes out a heavy sigh as he shuts and locks the door. "Look, Ingrid, I'm sorry you think I'm ogling you. You're...you're a beautiful girl, so talented, so...so everything that I could ever ask for. I thought I was reading some signals, maybe I misread..." He ran a hand through his hair. "So forgive me if I'm beating a dead horse here. Because I really, really like you, and I'm not so good at these sorts of things. Would you still like to come with me tomorrow, to the concert?"

Oh shoot. The concert. Tomorrow. Now that the protest has failed, and we're all confined to our dorms tonight, that only leaves tomorrow to retrieve the book. If the Collective decides that I can live. If we're still able to get into the library. If we're not all dead by then.

I press my head against the door frame. "I...I don't know."

"Ingrid."

"I don't think I can." I want to be straight with him because he deserves the truth. "Wil, and Jia, and Misty, we have...something planned."

"Something planned. And when were you going to tell me that? Were you just not going to show up?"

"No, I—"

"I get that friendships are important. But, and I don't mean to sound selfish here, what do I have to do to earn a place in your schedule?"

You have to be one of us. You have to show proof that you can shoot fire from your eyes, or read my thoughts and know that all I want is for everyone to be safe.

He does neither of these things. When I don't answer, he bursts out of the building and I have no choice but to follow, as he is the only way I can get back inside my dorm.

In Rita House, the security guard is startled awake by our unquiet trampling up the stairs. I scamper up quickly so he does not catch a glimpse of my face. But what does it matter? I've been gone for a half hour or more. The cameras will show this. Everyone I hold dear could be gone by morning, and I wasted it all on…on a boy I'm ridiculously infatuated with.

Ethan leads the way down the corridor. I have to run to keep up with him. He mutters to himself and leans against the wall beside my door, waiting for me to catch up to him.

"I'm sorry," I say.

"No…it's…forget about it." He swipes the card and doesn't meet my gaze. "Good night, Ingrid."

He turns on his heels and is down the hallway before I find the courage to respond. The door is held ajar by my hand only—running after him means I wouldn't be able to get into my room without winning him back to my side.

I push the door open and stride inside. I've taken too many risks for one night. The door startles me as it slams shut. I kick off my flip-flops and try to check my email, but the Internet is out. Probably a punishment for my transgressions. How am I supposed to get in touch with my parents? *Dad, I hope I didn't just kill you with my reckless teenage hormones.*

I'm too angry to go to sleep, but I'm too afraid of trying to escape my dorm once more. I call to Wil in my mind and pray that he can hear me. I get no response. Frustrated with my inability to act, and even more frustrated with my previous actions, I fall on my bed and drift into an uneasy slumber.

CHAPTER 10

Ingrid, someone is coming for you.

I draw a sharp breath. My tongue is like sandpaper. "Sunni?"

THUMP. THUMP. Two swift, authoritative knocks pierce the air. Throwing off the blankets I'd unconsciously covered myself with in the night, I feel wildly, emotionally outside myself as the sunlight assaults my eyes. The alarm clock blares 10:00 a.m.

"Ingrid? I'm coming in."

Good luck with that, I start to say, but the doorknob twists and the door opens.

Wil scans the room before entering, as if he's expecting someone else to be present. His gaze falls over my broken instruments and sympathy briefly touches his eyes. He juts his chin at the camera, and I detect a faint whirring sound as it's temporarily disabled, or rerouted.

"The Collective trashed your instruments?"

I grit my teeth. "Yes."

"You didn't tell us."

It's not important, I'm about to say, even though that's a lie. I change the subject, frowning. "How—?"

"All tutorials and meetings are cancelled today," he says before I can get my question out. "And any punishment that President Dean inflicted on students who went to the protest has been lifted."

"What? But why?"

"Officially? The protest 'worked' and President Dean is now meeting with the professors and other university shareholders to discuss the issues that Laura raised. She's fine, by the way. Shaken after a heavy meeting with some of the professors, including Ms. Agailya, but I was able to be nearby to calm her, and *help* her say the right things." There's more he's not saying—considering Laura's infatuation with him, I can only guess that he was nearer to her than he wanted to be. "She's sleeping in her room now. Unofficially..." He leans against the wall. "I think the Collective is discussing what to do with you."

"That's what Jadore said would happen. One of her cronies is supposed to come get me sometime today, and then the Collective will decide my fate." I reach for my cell phone on the nightstand. "My father..."

"Probably fine. No doubt Jadore would've rubbed it in your face if she had killed him."

I draw a deep breath. I wish I could reach my parents. "But I—"

"Spoke up during the protest. Aroused suspicion with your song."

I grip my duvet as I slowly sit down on the bed. "Jadore wasn't fooled anyway. She knew the whole protest had something to do with me, or us. When she escorted me here yesterday, she said that the Collective might decide to dissect me. Tonight."

"Then we have to get into the library as soon as possible. Assuming that Campbell's treatise is still there?"

"I haven't had any dreams telling me it isn't."

"I guess we'll have to trust that, then." His brow furrows as the wheels behind those dark brown eyes turn. "I...came to talk to you about something else."

I have a feeling I know what this conversation is going to be about, and exactly how it will play out. I curl my legs under my chin. "Yes?"

He looks about as uncomfortable as I feel. "I...I sensed that you weren't in your room last night."

I throw him a dirty look. "What about it?"

"It's not my intention to intrude on your personal life, Ingrid. I know it's none of my business. But sometimes, given what I have"—he points to his shaven head—"I can't really help it. You reached out to me last night. I heard, felt, my name in your thoughts. And so I felt you move from this spot, across campus. With Ethan."

I can't meet his gaze. My cheeks are burning up. "I don't want to talk about it."

"Neither do I. So I'm gonna tell you a story instead." He crosses his arms. "When I was in junior high, there was this girl. Camilla. Very pretty. Prettiest in the class, I thought. Had very little control over my telepathy at the time, which often got me into trouble at school and at home. Anyway. Me and Camilla had one class together. Biology. And I sat right behind her, and well, um, there's a reason I'm not a biology major. Didn't learn a thing in that class." He looks mildly embarrassed. "In the first week of class, she kept giving me dirty looks. The whole class. Every ten minutes or so, she'd turn around, give me the stink eye, and turn back around. I don't know if she knew that I caught her gaze every single time. Turns out, the whole week I'd been broadcasting thoughts to her, and her alone. Inappropriate thoughts for the classroom. She thought she was crazy. Thought I was crazy. She transferred out of that school by the end of the month. Never heard from her again."

My eyes widen. "And she didn't tell anyone? No one got suspicious about your powers?"

"People latch on to reasonable, logical explanations for things," he replies. "Some teachers swore they heard me talking in class all the time, and I'd get sent to the office, but I would get a slap on the hand because my grades were so high. My classmates would get confused about why the teacher was picking on me, so I'd be pitied rather than teased. Most of the time." He shakes his head. "Anyway. I'm telling you this because even though I'm better at controlling myself now, it's the reason I can't be in a relationship, not with anyone. Not even..."

He can't say her name, so I say it for him. "Kimberly."

Wil doesn't look surprised, but I have piqued his curiosity. "How did you know?"

"Jia told me."

"Hmm." He sits next to me on the bed and stretches out his long legs. "Look, Ingrid, I'm not going to tell you what's right or what's wrong about this stuff. I'm just saying that it's easier not to get involved with someone who isn't a Spark. And it's easiest to be alone."

"But you're not alone. Not really. You have all of us."

He nods, slowly. "Yes. And sometimes even that's too much."

"You can feel what we feel...all the time, can't you?"

"Sometimes. Feeling other people's emotions is one of the things I haven't completely mastered yet. But I see you've successfully sidetracked me from talking about Ethan."

I draw a deep, anxiety-cleansing breath. "I guess I did."

"He doesn't know anything about us, right?"

"Of course not."

"But you were on the verge of telling him." He sighs. "He's too close with Ms. Agailya. You know he sees a psychiatrist every week, right?"

"He told me, yeah." I frown. "But he told me that in confidence. How did you—?"

"He's on my floor, and we talk sometimes. Followed his energy one day because he was allowed to miss tutorial. Wanted to make sure he wasn't being...*transferred.*"

"Wil, he's not..." I want to phrase this question carefully. "He's not a Spark like us, is he?"

He looks as if I just asked him what colour he was. "What? No. Why would you ask that?"

"He says he's on a special diet. And sometimes he doesn't remember things. And he did *not* look well the other day. Sort of like how I felt when I ate the food here."

Wil considers this. "How long has he felt that way?"

"Not sure. But he says he's had memory problems his whole life."

"I'm not sure what sort of power would manifest with those symptoms." He shoves his hands in his pockets dismissively and saunters for the door, but I can see his face. He's flipping scenarios and calculating variables.

"If he is a Spark," I say, "I shouldn't let him out of my sight. I need to keep him close, in case Jadore—"

"There's something else you're not telling me." He leans one hand against the wall. "Wait a minute. Weren't you supposed to do something with him tonight? And that's why you wanted to go the library yesterday?"

My teeth sink into my lip. I can't hide the truth from Wil. It's impossible. I stare at my bare feet. "I told him that I might not be able to make it."

"That's probably for the best, Ingrid. We all have to make sacrifices, you know."

He twists the doorknob and I catch his face—and immediately I know he's not talking about the sacrifices I have to make. There's another girl's name written all over him, and he pulls open the door with the pent-up frustration of someone who wants what he can't have.

"What should I tell Jia if she asks about you?"

He stops in the doorway. His expression is pained. "She asked about me?"

"You know she always thinks of you."

He sighs and with the flick of his finger reactivates the camera in my room and then shuts the door behind him.

It's getting late in the afternoon and I'm not interested in waiting around for someone to dole out my fate. Who knows if anyone from the Collective will come? Everyone else is wandering around campus—I see people lounging under trees from my window. Perhaps the Collective has decided to let me live.

I still can't get a hold of my parents. Despite what Wil said, my father could be dead by now. My stomach tightens. I could appeal to the faceless man from my dreams, but speaking to him, much less finding his book, seems further away now than it ever has been.

Jia texts, saying she is at the Sparkstone Bakery. I tell her I will meet her there in five minutes.

Glaring at the camera, I fetch my purse. "I'm hungry. I'm just going to get some food. If you're going to kill me, poisoning the food might be an apt choice."

There is, of course, no response.

The door is unlocked, either by Wil or Ethan's doing. Cameras follow me down the hallway, but no aliens in disguise appear, and the security guard at the desk gives me the briefest passing glance as I leave Rita House. Nerves swim in my stomach as I near the bakery. This is the second time I have left my room since Jadore told me not to. I hold my cell phone up to the sky—no reception. *Please, please let my parents be okay.*

The bell rings above the Sparkstone Bakery door as I step inside, but my nerves have devoured my hunger, leaving me sated yet jittery. Jia has already ordered, and she cradles her untouched croissant in a napkin in her right hand. She looks afraid to eat it. The bakery is the only cheap, fast place left to grab lunch, besides the handful of restaurants that share supplies with the university cafeteria. If the bakery becomes contaminated—if it isn't already—the grocery store will be the only place left to buy non-drugged food. Unless they start pumping Gen-Grow into the fruit and vegetables. Then we're in trouble for sure.

A crowd of hungry students stands in the corner by the window, waiting in line, and I step aside to let them know they can go in front of me as I approach Jia. "Where're Misty and Wil?"

"I don't know where Misty is. I sent her a text, but I haven't heard from her since yesterday."

Since the protest. An uncomfortable knot tightens my stomach. "Maybe Wil knows where she is."

Jia shrugs. "She'll turn up. She always does."

"We need a better system for organizing..." I peter off as Jia moves to make way for another hungry customer. The two girls behind the counter glare at us—we're in the way of business. I gesture to the door, and we reconvene on the wooden patio, where students and Sparkstone workers bask in the sun and eat their lunches. Their gaze passes over me but there is no recognition in their eyes. Perhaps I am safe, for the moment. "I mean, why don't we just text each other and agree to meet at a specific place?"

"Because that's traceable," Jia replies. She sniffs her croissant warily and tears off a small piece, then offers me some. I shake my head, and she savours the pastry. "Wil makes the meetings. It's the safest way. I...I trust him."

I frown. "You *trust* him."

"Of course I do. Don't you?"

"No, yeah, I do, but the way you're saying it..."

"What?" Her voice is laced with worry and defensiveness.

I cross my arms and smile. "It's okay, Jia. You can tell me."

"Tell you what?" She laughs nervously and looks up at the awning, as if searching for a camera that doesn't exist.

"You like Wil."

She stuffs the rest of her croissant in her mouth to avoid responding.

"Fine. I won't bring it up," I say, leaning back warily in the patio chair, scanning the street for Collective agents.

Two men in maintenance uniforms stride down the sidewalk on the other side of the road. I turn my head and shield my face with my hand, hoping they don't recognize me. "But communication between all of us, it's not great. We should do something about that."

She chews on her croissant for a few minutes, and when it's down, she perches on the chair and rests her chin on her knees. "Any mark we leave is evidence of who we really are. The Collective could come at any moment and take us away. And not just us. Jadore has shown you especially that our families are not safe. That is why we cannot meet as often as we should, and that is why we cannot communicate, except in person, and via Wil."

I keep my voice low until the maintenance men are out of sight. "I know, I get that. But we're not going to be very effective as a team if we can't get together and—"

Jia interrupts me quietly. "I think we showed our effectiveness at the protest."

I squeeze her arm. "We can do better. And it wasn't a complete failure. I…" I glance around to make sure no one is listening and then drop my voice. "I *saw* him there."

Though fear paints her porcelain face, her eyes brighten. "Joseph G. Campbell?"

"Yes. Something about the music, it called him."

"We have to tell Wil and Misty right away," she says. "Can you replicate the sound? Call him again?"

"I…I don't know. I was playing last night, and nothing happened. It just seemed like all of the pieces came together in that one moment in the cafeteria, and he sort of appeared—not completely, but if I had played longer in that one specific moment, if Jadore hadn't interrupted—"

"She saw him too then. That's what she was swinging at."

"Yeah."

Jia sinks into the chair, thinking. "I wish Sunni were here. She would tell us what to do next."

"We have to find Campbell's treatise. That's what she would've wanted us to do." I stand. "And we don't have much time. Jadore said that the Collective is deciding my fate today. And the restricted section is being gutted tomorrow. All of the books are going to be moved or destroyed. At least, that's what happened in my dream. We have to sneak in tonight."

"Tonight? But we can't stage another distraction—"

"Forget about the distraction. We'll have Wil with us, and the alien bracelets. We'll just have to hope that...that nothing bad happens."

"And what about your father? My family? If Jadore catches us, the Collective will not hesitate to harm them."

"Don't you see?" I gesture to the Sparkstone campus before us. "They're going to kill us anyway eventually. I'm already trying to avoid Jadore's agents right now. If we don't at least try to figure out who Campbell is, what Sunni's fascination with him was, and what the Collective is really trying to do here with us, our families won't be the only ones who will suffer. Sparkstone isn't the only school that the Collective has its fingers in."

Jia takes a deep breath and closes her eyes. "I know you're right, Ingrid. It makes sense, in my head. But my heart. If it were my sister, and not your father who was sitting in the hospital on the brink of death, I would not be so brave."

"Thanks," I say quietly. "My mum and dad are all I have. I..." There's a sob welling in my throat, but I swallow it. Now is not the time for tears. "They've always taught me to go after what I want, to stand up for what's right. I think if I didn't at least take the risk, I would be disregarding everything they've taught me."

Jia is not as shy with her tears. She stands and embraces me. "Then we must be brave for both of our families, and all of the families behind every student here."

I return the embrace. It's been a long time since I've had a real friend, someone whom I could talk to like this. Even though Sparkstone has brought me great pain, I'm grateful that I have found someone, no—more than that—a group of friends that I can trust and that trusts me to bear it.

When Jia pulls away, the grief has faded from her expression. She is the determined, quiet warrior I have grown to know. "I'll find Wil."

I smile. "All right. I'll find Misty. Where should we meet?"

Dark rain clouds obscure the sun in the late afternoon sky. Jia looks to the library. "My room, in a half hour. Wil can secure it."

Jia's room. Right. At least if a bunch of hafelglob show up to take me away, I will be well defended. And if someone shows up before that? "I'll text you if I have problems."

She looks mildly uncomfortable with the idea, but she nods. "I'll see you soon."

CHAPTER 11

Finding Misty is not as easy a task as I thought it would be. She's not in her room. I knock a bunch of times and try her cell—nothing. I check Rogers Hall and look into the cafeteria, even though it's not open yet. I even think about going to the library, but I highly doubt that she's in there.

I'm not sure, but I think I'm being followed. Men in maintenance uniforms sprout up like weeds around every turn. They keep their distance, seemingly more interested in watching than advancing. As I enter Rita House once more, I dial my mother's number but my cell phone lacks a dial tone. I've been cut off completely.

I glance behind me. Three maintenance workers converge in the lobby, levelling me with unblinking stares. I race up the stairs to the second floor to try Misty's room again. They don't follow.

The second-floor hallway is much like the third-floor hallway, but on closer inspection, I notice the walls have been bruised with dark ashy spots, as if someone had punched them recently with a hot iron. Only one girl has fists that can generate that sort of heat.

"Misty?" I yell, running down the hallway, following the trail of burned spots. It stops in front of the girls' communal bathroom. Fearing the worst, I push the bathroom door open and find that I'm not alone.

Misty is perched on the open window ledge. Her body is shaking, almost uncontrollably. She's sobbing. Startled by the door, she gasps and falls forward.

I scream and run for the window. Her icy white-knuckled hand squeezes the ledge, almost freezing her grip in place. Misty dangles helplessly on the side of the building, struggling to bring her other hand around. I grab the hand holding on to the ledge and pull, ignoring the frosty cold biting my fingers.

"No...stop..." But her pleas don't sound sincere. She is the picture of fear as she looks up at me. Her face says, *I don't want to die.*

"Give me your hand!" I say, reaching for it. She flails it and I grab hold. Her boots kick the side of the building, and I get a good look at how far the fall would be. Two floors. Concrete paths line the base of the building.

Bracing my feet against the wall, I heave with every ounce of strength I have. Misty grunts as I pull her arms up. I'm out of breath. My heart is racing. I get her up far enough so that she can climb back in the window, but I'm afraid to let her go.

Her lips are trembling. She turns again to the window, but I'm faster. I knock the support out and slam and latch the window shut before she can even think of trying again.

I don't know what to say. All I can do is stare at her with surprise. With sympathy. With...disgust.

This makes her angry. "Get off me," she mutters, throwing away my grip. She backs up against a bathroom stall and buries her face in her hands.

"Misty, I'm…" I'm sorry? No, I just saved her life. She was going to kill herself. I can't be sorry for that, or my reaction. "What were you thinking?"

"Leave me alone!" she shouts, but the words are muffled by her sobs and her hands.

"No."

She goes to the window again, but instead of opening it, she starts banging on the wall beside it, screaming. There's a lock on the bathroom door, and I twist it so that no one can come in. Then I check for cameras. There's one in the center of the ceiling, but it looks as though it's been fried. Seems that Misty didn't want the Collective to see her demise either. For the moment, I am also out of the Collective's gaze.

The banging stops. One hand is smouldering red, as if it's about to explode into flames. The other is white, frostbitten. The wall bares burn marks and cries water as the ice melts. Her forehead rests against the damage. "Why didn't you just let me fall?"

"Why would I?"

"Because I ain't got… ain't got nothin'."

"Double negative. You know you have us."

"I…" She turns, slowly, and slides down the wall. "I don't have Sunni."

I step cautiously towards her. I wonder how long it will take the Collective to figure out the camera is broken. I listen for thundering footsteps in the hallway, but all I hear is some rock music playing in the next room, and the laughter of girls a few doors down.

I take a chance and sit down next to her. She does not protest. I mull over a couple of different things to say but end up discarding them all. With Misty, silence is my trump card—the one thing she cannot chide me for, not really. Misty picks at the remaining black nail polish on her forefinger and takes a deep, choked breath.

"I loved her," Misty whispers.

"Seems like you were all really close," I reply. "If I had gotten to know her better—"

"No." Misty cuts me off and lays a shaking hand on my knee. It's scorching hot. Her fingernails are bit down to the cuticle. Her breath is wobbly. "I really *loved* her." Then, much quieter: "So goddamn much."

Oh.

I slump slowly against the wall. Misty's staring into a distant memory. She removes her hand from my knee and cracks a few knuckles to fill the silence.

"Did . . . did you tell her?" I ask.

Misty shakes her head. "I didn't know how."

"Was she also . . . ?" I want to leave the word unsaid, not because it feels wrong to say but because it feels heavy on my tongue. "Was she gay?"

Her eyes narrow. "I hate that term. People think they can just put a label on me all the time, so that it's *easier* to get me. I loved Sunni because . . . because she was the one person in my life who understood me. She was there for me when no one else was."

"Sorry, I didn't mean to—"

"I know you didn't." The harshness of her tone is lost in a sob. "I will never love anyone else as much as I loved her. Ever. She was . . . everything to me."

She buries her face in her hands and leans against me. Carefully, afraid to anger or upset her further, I wrap an arm around her and draw her closer. She doesn't resist.

"I want to kill Jadore," she hisses through her tears. "But maybe it would be better if I just went Sunni's way."

I squeeze her. "Sunni wouldn't want that. She'd want you to live. She'd want you to fight for all the students here."

Misty sniffs and wipes her nose on her knees. "I know. But after what happened yesterday, it's like...like there's no friggin' hope left. How am I supposed to go on when I've got nothin' to go on for?"

I purse my lips. "I think I should show you something."

She frowns as I stand up and lead her out of the bathroom. She follows me reluctantly. Her shoulders are hunched, and her eyes dart around like a scared mouse worried that a predator will swoop down at any moment and end her life.

"Don't tell no one about this," she says.

"I won't."

Misty nods. No additional threats, no angry glares. Just a simple, vulnerable nod.

I take her to my room. Upon crossing the threshold, Misty crosses her arms and takes a deep breath. Right. Coming here is hard for her. The camera's red light is barely visible to the naked eye, but it's there all the same, the invulnerable Eye of Sauron, watching us. I draw an unsteady breath. Would the Collective dare to fetch me now that I'm with Misty, who is unstable enough as it is? One wrong move and she'd burn us all.

Digging into my pocket, I gesture for Misty to go into the bathroom. "It's there if you need it."

She frowns at me but notices the slight tilt in my eyebrows and doesn't argue. She shuts the door after her, and I quickly text Jia to tell her I've found Misty and that we'll be along to her room shortly. Then I pull out a clean towel from the bottom dresser drawer. I knock once on the bathroom door, and when I hear no protest, I open the door with the towel in hand and slip inside. I don't close the door all the way so it's not as suspicious—for all the Collective knows, I'm calming Misty down in a private bathroom and convincing her to take a shower.

Misty sits on the edge of the toilet. I place the towel on the vanity while I turn on the shower, and then move the top of the toilet tank aside. The mirror steams up quickly.

"Okay, what's going on?"

"Sorry about all this." I grimace as I roll up my sleeves and plunge my hand into the water to retrieve the plastic bag. I unseal it to reveal Sunni's journal and wait to see if Misty recognizes the book on sight—her reaction does not change.

"What is it?" The edge in her voice has returned.

"It's Sunni's," I say, and hand her the journal.

Misty examines it closely and opens the cover a crack. She closes it just as quickly, as if peeking inside Sunni's collection of words is sacrilege. "Where did you get this?"

"Joseph G. Campbell sent it to me."

She lowers her gaze to the book once more and takes a deep breath. "Did you read it?"

I bite my lip. "I...I skimmed it. Whoever this Joseph G. Campbell is, he seems to want me to keep it safe. I think...Misty, I think this is the reason that Sunni died."

Her eyes widen. "Did she write about us in here? About our...powers?"

I nod. "That, and other things. Snippets of dreams. Sketches of Joseph G. Campbell. She was trying to figure out who he was."

"Sounds like you did more than just skim it."

I sigh in exasperation. "Fine. I read bits of it. I didn't mean to pry. But I think Sunni would've wanted me—*us*—to continue her work. Through this journal and my dreams, I found out that Campbell's treatise is in the library. I think Joseph G. Campbell is behind all of this—the Collective, the harvesting. But somewhere along the line, his motives got twisted. It seems like his intentions were good."

The journal rests squarely on Misty's legs. The struggle is written plainly on her face: to open it, or to leave its secrets in peace. Eventually she sets it on the vanity. "I don't know who this Joseph G. Campbell alien is, but I don't trust anything that isn't human. Especially if he's the one really responsible for Sunni's death."

"Jadore was responsible for Sunni's death. She seems to have her own agenda."

She doesn't argue with that. Instead, she takes out her phone, and her thumbs fly rapidly over the screen.

"What are you doing?" I ask.

She screws up her lips. "Texting Sunni."

"Oh. Okay."

The question hangs in my voice, and Misty rolls her eyes. "I know. It's dumb. And her phone is probably with the Collective, and the aliens might be readin' everything I send. Don't care, though. Not like they can understand the language anyway. It just…helps."

I peer over her shoulder, and I don't recognize the language.

"Made up," she whispers. "Changin' syntax, and there's about three or four different words for every English word. Sometimes I throw in a Spanish and a Russian word randomly, just to keep them on their toes. I...I made it up with Sunni one time. Long time ago. She wouldn't really be able to read it anyway, but I just like to pretend she can."

"That's...really sweet." Leaning against the vanity, I exhale slowly. "I'm sorry I didn't show you this sooner. I was just a little scared of Wil's rule about not writing stuff down."

Misty snorts. "Yeah. That's kinda a serious rule."

I'm not sure whether she's being serious or sarcastic, so I continue. "I think it's time I showed this to Jia and Wil. They're waiting in Jia's room." I grip the vanity tightly. "But if you think we shouldn't go prying into Sunni's personal things, I'll understand. I just think it will help us track down Joseph G. Campbell faster, which, despite what you might think of him, I think will help us avenge Sunni's death and put a stop to all the deaths the Collective is causing."

She chews on my words. "You think that this book will help us bring down the Collective."

I muster up my confidence. "Jadore hates Campbell with a passion. This I know for sure. And if she hates him that much—even if Campbell is part of the Collective— well, the enemy of our enemy is our friend."

Misty grips the journal. It shakes with her trembling grip. "Sunni didn't ever deserve no enemies." She stands, waving the journal in my face. "I hope you're right about all this."

Me too. I nod. "Let's go."

"I was starting to get worried. Where *were* you guys?" Jia asks as she shuts the door of her room.

"Just took me a little longer than I thought to find Misty. Sorry."

Wil raises an eyebrow—he can sense I'm withholding something—but he does not comment. Probably because Misty is challenging him with a death stare.

"So. Ideas for the library heist?" Wil says instead.

Misty glances at me, and then holds up Sunni's journal. "You wanna show them this now, or after we come up with a new plan to break into Sparkstone library's restricted section?"

"What's that?" Jia asks.

"Sunni's journal," I reply.

Wil stands up defensively. "No. No, no no—"

"Yes, yes, yes," I say. "She broke your rule. It might be the thing that made the Collective come after her in the first place, but it also could contain the clues, or even the answers, to our questions about Joseph G. Campbell."

"And you've read it, I assume," Wil says flatly. "That's why the Collective came after you, destroyed your room. The aliens were looking for *that*. You've brought it here to Jia's room, putting *her* in danger."

Jia flushes red from Wil's concern and then says, "The Collective trashed your room?"

"Instruments mostly," Misty mutters. I throw her a defensive glare. She shrugs. "What? I was just there. Don't think I didn't notice."

I hold my ground. "Yeah. They didn't find the journal, so...so that's what's important." Jia does not hide her sympathy, but I shake my head. If I start thinking about my mangled instruments, I won't be able to focus on the mission. "Sunni knew she was going to die. She could see the future in her dreams. Whether she died because she wrote stuff down, or just because she asked too many questions about Joseph G. Campbell I don't know, but she knew it was going to happen, and she spent her last few days making sure that we would be able to retrace her steps through her visions, through the research she did, so that we could discover the things she knew."

Wil sits back down on the bed. "I don't like this."

"No one asked if you *liked* it," Misty retorts. "Ingrid read it and it's the thing that's going to lead us to Campbell, and god knows what else."

"It's quarter after seven," Wil says. "We should go before it gets too late."

My teeth sink into my lower lip. I wonder about the hafelglob in disguise down in the lobby, if they've been given orders to take me away yet. Misty tosses me the journal and shoves her hands on her hips. "Fine. I'll go in there and find the stupid book."

"That wasn't the original plan," I say. "We're supposed to work together on this."

"Screw that. Wil's already refused to accept this"—she points to the journal—"and Jia? Invisible girl can't get past the motion detectors without Wil's help, which he's already made clear he's not interested in givin'—"

"I didn't say that," Wil says defensively. "I fixed the bands. I risked my life to find out about Gen-Grow and Substance 454. I've given *plenty* to this whole operation."

"Oh sure. Mr. Rules. Who put *you* in charge, anyway? Why should we listen to you? Goin' off on your own, doing your own little heists. You think you're *so* smart, you think you don't need us."

Clare C. Marshall

"Not true. This is why I don't invite you along. We'd have hafelglob and god knows what else on us in a heartbeat if you were involved in every single mission."

"Guys, please—" Jia holds up her hands to intervene, but Misty holds up a fiery hand of her own.

"You're the worst of it, too," Misty spits at Jia. "Always going along with what Wil says, like he's the paragon of—"

"Stop it, Misty. You're just being mean, now," Jia says, her face a brilliant red.

"Mean? You want to know mean? I can show you…"

The three of them descend into a screaming match and forget I'm here. Well, not if I can help it. My grip on Sunni's journal tightens, and I whisper a prayer to the gods of aim and accuracy as I throw it at the opposite wall. It hits the dresser next to the bathroom door with a furious *bang* and then tumbles to the carpet, dented but otherwise intact.

Misty fixes a death stare on me. "What. Did. You. Just—?"

"I just realized that our biggest problem might not even be the Collective," I say, crossing the room to retrieve the journal. "The Collective is up there in space, biding its time, because it knows that one of these days, we'll kill each other before it even gets a chance. That's when it'll swoop in and harvest our precious genes. We'll have done all the hard work for the aliens."

Misty starts to protest, but I retrieve the journal and hold it up.

"We can't lose sight that we're in this together," I say. "We have to be there for each other, or else this"—I swirl the journal between the four of us—"won't work."

The three of them consider my words. Wil nods sagely.

Jia, embarrassed, is trying not to tear up. Misty screws her lip and bites her nail, avoiding my gaze.

"All four of us are going to the library. And all four of us are going to fight whatever comes our way. No matter what." I stress the last point while looking at Jia because she knows just as well as I that the consequences are dire.

I can almost hear Wil thinking, he looks so pensive. "The bands will make suits for us again. That should help, somewhat. And the motion sensors shouldn't be a problem, not with the adjustments I've made."

Wil, Jia, and Misty discuss the details of the new plan to break into the restricted section of the library. I listen, of course, and make suggestions, but my mind wanders. I'm giving up Ethan's concert to do this. I hate this. I hate that I'm sacrificing my potential relationship with Ethan for finding an old book in the restricted section of the library. Guilt smoulders in my stomach like a hungry flame. The lives of the students here are more important than some date with a cute guy. Even if that cute guy is Ethan.

I wish I had the courage to tell him our secret. Then he could just come along on the raid. I imagine us breaking into the library together and finding the tome, and all five of us destroying Jadore. And then somehow, Sunni's spirit descends from the heavens to congratulate us, and Wil works his science-magic to engineer Sunni a new body...

"Hey. Focus." Misty snaps a finger in front of my face, breaking me out of my fantasy. "You ready to go or what?"

"Yeah. Ready."

CHAPTER 12

A few bleary-eyed students in the library hover over laptops and thick tomes, and they don't notice us as we creep by. Not that they can see us anyway, not while we exist in Jia's watery, invisible world. Things take on a fluid quality here. It's as if we are walking through a living watercolour painting. Sounds are more striking and lance the ears as diamond would strike and shatter glass.

The aliens in human form in the Rita House lobby didn't notice us slip away either. They seemed agitated about their assigned post, and one grumbled about how other patrols all over campus had reported no sign of me. A group of three disguised aliens stormed up the stairs just as we disappeared outside.

The lights are dimmer near the restricted section. There are more signs on the door today, warning students that the section is going to be gutted tomorrow morning, and that the noise might disrupt everyone's studies. No sign of any hafelglob here, not yet anyway. There's a keypad with a swipe machine next to the door. The black box makes me nervous. I wish I had Ethan's stolen master key card right now.

Let me just try something, Wil says.

Squeezing Jia's hand—she flushes a bright shade of red, which glows in the blue hues surrounding us—Wil presses his palm against the key card reader and squeezes his eyes shut. The veins in his temples flare up temporarily but recede when the keypad flashes green and dings. The door before us clicks. Unlocked.

Jia opens the door slowly, and one by one we file in. Once the door shuts, there's a faint beeping sound, and the door locks once more.

Wil steps forward into the dark hallway before us. "Odd," he says. "No cameras in here."

"No lights either," Misty says, and a small fire appears in her palm.

"Don't set off any fire detectors," I mutter, smiling.

Misty half smiles, and the flame dims.

We tread down the hallway. It's not the lack of cameras that I find odd about this long hallway—it's that it slopes downward. We walk until I'm fairly certain we're underground. That wouldn't be odd if I was sure that we were entering a basement, but the steep descent suggests something *deeper* than a basement, which worries me even more. There are no doors, and no lights lining the hallway. Eventually, after Wil confirms that we're alone, Jia releases us from her invisibility so we can use the wall for support.

"A couple more feet, then I think there's a door up ahead," Wil says.

"It's kind of weird that the Collective actually cares about books, you know?" Misty says. "I mean, they're just books. Written by humans, probably. Why would they build an entire section just for them?"

I shrug. "For appearances?"

She frowns. "I dunno. Just doesn't seem like something they'd do."

"Maybe there are books here written by people on other planets," Jia says, running her hand along the rough wall.

"Misty has a point," Wil says. "The Collective wouldn't build something like this and then use resources to transport books here unless it was planning to use it for an explicit purpose."

"In my dream, it seemed so normal that it was here. I mean, except for the part where parts of the library get destroyed, and there's a giant eye watching everything. And Sunni, telling me to go through it."

"Go through the eye?" Jia scrunches up her face in disgust.

"Yeah, I'm not sure if that's supposed to mean something. But she's been telling me to go through doors a lot."

"Eyes are windows to the soul," Wil says.

"The main, recurring part of the dream is about me going through a door of some kind. But her telling me about Campbell's treatise, that's pretty recent. Maybe the Collective knows that Campbell's book is here."

"Jadore would've found it by now if she knew it was here and would be keeping it somewhere else, more secure, like, not with other books," Misty mutters.

She holds up her hand-flame as I flip through Sunni's journal to the page with the reference number. "*13042-4826*. It's weird that it even has a reference number, if that's the case."

"You said that Campbell has a way of hiding Sunni's journal from the Collective. Maybe it's the same with his treatises. They're meant to be found by those who truly need them," Jia says.

"Here we go," Wil says.

I hear Wil opening a door with no difficulty, and green light fills the hallway. Misty's fire goes out and I shade my eyes as we file into the room.

An eerie green light cascades from the ceiling. We're certainly underground, so the light coming through the green ceiling-wide, stained-glass window above us is not from the sky. I feel as if we're actually on an alien spaceship that's been transformed into an antique library. For all we know, this could be exactly where we are.

One thing is for certain, however: I've seen this library before. In my dreams.

"No wonder this place is restricted," Wil mutters. "It's like Oz up in this business."

I chuckle. "If only there were a yellow brick road to take us to the book."

"You have the reference number. What is it again?" Jia asks.

I check the bookmarked page once more. "*13042-4826.*"

"Right." Wil claps his hands together, and the sound echoes in the quiet library. "Let's get to this, then."

We scour the aisles while Wil scouts further ahead. Against one end of the wall is a series of doors with numbers on them.

"Must be in this room," he says. "Reference numbers *13000-4000* to *13000-5000.*"

Misty bunches up her sleeve and tries the doorknob. Unlocked.

"They really don't care about security back here," she remarks.

"Probably because they don't expect anyone to be back here," Jia says.

Wil looks more concerned. *There doesn't seem to be anything of value here so far. I suppose that's why it's getting cleared out tomorrow. Still, we can't let our guard down.*

As the door creaks open, he sticks his head into the dark room. "It's clean."

We pile inside the musty, dark room. Misty's hand lights up in flame, and Wil bolts the door shut. Jia finds a single light bulb in the middle of the room and pulls the long cord dangling from the ceiling. The bulb flickers on, Misty's flame dies, and we see the true work that lies ahead of us. The book isn't inside a secure glass case, or in a safe locked in an office. Because instead of organized shelves, this room is filled with boxes. Some are stacked and sealed with tape, while others lie open and half empty. It looks as though whoever was in charge of unpacking these books left when the job was halfway done. If Sunni's reference number is correct, Campbell's treatise is in one of these many boxes. Hiding in plain sight is the best security—the kind that the Collective has mastered. Whether someone in the Collective has purposely hidden Campbell's treatise, or Campbell himself is leading us on a wild goose chase, one thing is certain: we will be in this room for hours looking through these boxes.

"I'll take these five," Wil says, pointing to the pile to the right of the door.

We fan out. I head towards the far right corner. These boxes aren't secured with tape, just folded shut. I open the first and my heart sinks even more—they're all textbooks of varying sizes and topics. Unpacking and repacking the box is going to take time that we don't have.

"You can't pinpoint the location of actual books, right?" I ask Wil.

He snorts. "Afraid it's technology and living things only."

"You haven't even tried?" Jia asks, already halfway through her box across from Wil.

"I have my hands full with abilities as it is. Have you tried turning things invisible by just looking at them?"

"I suppose not."

Misty dumps a box of books onto the floor. The clattering noise sends my stomach into a nervous state.

"What are you doing?" I say through my teeth.

"More efficient," she mumbles as she picks up a book, glances at the title, then messily places it back in the empty box.

Wil's eyes widen. "Not really! There's no one here now, but the hafelglob could be—"

I freeze and listen. Somewhere behind the closed door, I hear the squishing sounds of something large and slimy trailing its way on tiled floor, towards us.

Hurry, Wil says. *I was distracted and they eluded my senses.*

I empty another two boxes as quickly and as quietly as I can, but I see no tome with the reference number that matches the one in Sunni's journal. It's hopeless. The slime noises are closer now. The hafelglob might be blind but they will sniff out our location in minutes.

"Might be a patrol," Misty whispers. "They *are* looking for Ingrid."

Or they figured out we were here, Wil says telepathically.

Misty's eyes flare with rage. "But we were careful!"

"And the Collective is smart. Jadore knew we were up to something. They probably sent patrols everywhere, and when they couldn't find us—"

Jia silences us by raising her hand. She reaches with her other to Wil, and together they become invisible. I blink. Misty disappears, and then a hand grabs my wrist and I'm yanked into the invisible world too.

Be very quiet, Wil warns.

The door opens and three hafelglob slither in. The green glow from the main library room casts a grotesque light on their slimy skin, revealing tiny indents and scars I'd never noticed before. They gurgle and squirm around us, and we maneuver awkwardly around them and the books on the floor. We are in a deadly dance, and if the enemy touches us, we lose.

Jia slips through the now-open door, and Wil slides out after her. The hafelglob are deep in the room now. We're almost in the clear.

Misty slips through, and then it's my turn. I hold my breath as I slip through the open doorway. It's a thin space. And I make it through—only to scuff my boot against the tile floor.

On top of that, I curse.

One of the hafelglob points all his tentacles towards us. Sniffing. It mutters something in its native, guttural tongue, and then, they dash towards us.

Run! Wil shouts.

Running while invisible is hard. We're all trying to hang on, and Wil has longer legs than Jia and Misty, and I'm clomping around, giving us all away. The hafelglob are on our tail now that they have our scent. Another one joins from behind a bookshelf, making it four in pursuit of four. What could be worse? I glance behind me again. Shoot. They're all wielding ray guns.

One fires, and a red dash of light zooms by my shoulder, narrowly missing me.

We have to split up. We'll be harder to follow, Wil says.

I don't disagree, but there's only one exit from this maze of bookshelves that we know of, and it could be blocked off already by an army of hafelglob and god knows what other aliens the Collective has in its service.

Break! Wil commands.

He lets go, and this immediately renders Misty and me visible and vulnerable. Misty's already firing up her ice and flame, and I tuck Sunni's journal under my arm, near my heart, ready to use it as a shield if I have to. Wil is visible for only a second before he disappears down an aisle of bookshelves.

I'm not letting myself be alone. I follow Misty down the adjacent row.

"What are you doing?" she hisses at me. "You're going to give me away!"

"I thought you might enjoy a challenge," I say, glancing over my shoulder. Sure enough, one hafelglob has found us and is quickly gaining. "Behind!"

I duck as Misty throws a flame ball larger than my head over me and towards the hafelglob. The fire hits several of its flailing tentacles and sears them clean off. The creature howls in pain, which signals our position.

Misty lets out a string of curses as she readies another flame. "Well? You on the lookout for this book or what?"

"Oh. Yes. Um . . ." I quickly scan the numbers as we whiz by. "Not this aisle."

"Could be any aisle. It wasn't in that stupid room."

She hurls her flame at the hafelglob behind us, who has slowed due to his injury. Damn it. She's right. I slow down momentarily and gaze at the books shelved at eye level. They're not in any kind of order—not alphabetical by author, not according to reference number or even topic. Everything has been ordered randomly. The Collective hadn't intended this library to be a library at all. It's a cover for something, and while these books are all real, they're just set dressing for something we don't know about yet.

As we near the end of the aisle, a dark figure appears, and Misty almost throws another ball of flame when I recognize Wil's glasses reflecting the green. I stay her hand just in time. Her power almost flies out of control, and she manages to send the ball hurling towards the wounded hafelglob behind us. An unpleasant *splat* sound results.

"Wait!" I hiss before Wil can take off again. "Don't go. We're stronger if we stick together."

I don't think that Wil will agree, but then I notice his right arm is steaming. A ray gun wound, but just a graze. He struggles to hide the pain in his face and nods curtly.

Together, the three of us take off down the next aisle. I glance at the books, hoping that the reference number will pop out at me in a brilliant light. "Where's Jia?"

She's close. Heading towards the exit. Wait. He pauses. *No, she's lost. But close.*

More slime sounds from the left. Misty takes the lead and I'm right behind her, with Wil bringing up the rear. Every corner we turn I keep expecting to be wrapped in tentacles, to be shoved down a throat of never-ending spiralling teeth. The sounds surround us until I'm no longer sure where they're coming from.

Use the band if you're scared, Wil says, his voice reassuring to my frightened mind.

I'm about to activate its defences when a rush of wind passes us. Jia briefly flashes in and out of the visible realm just as four hafelglob surround us. They all have ray guns, and they shoot at us from all angles. I'm huddled in the middle, hugging Sunni's journal to my chest, counting seconds until I die painfully. Misty throws fire and ice at the hafelglob but tonight, for this particular batch of hafelglob, she's not fast enough. They dash between her blows.

Misty is not a machine. Sweat runs down her brow. Her hair is soaked, and her hands are shaking. She screams her fatigue. She will fight to the bitter end if she has to. She pauses for just a second to take a breath, but that's the one second the alien has been waiting for. It aims its ray gun and fires. My eyes widen. The blast is heading straight for her chest.

"Misty! Watch—"

My words are slower than my movements. I dive in front of Misty as the shot hits me square in the chest and sends us flying backward. We hit the floor in a pile, and Jia rushes to our side to hide us. Before she can, Misty scrambles to her feet with a wild look on her face. Not because I just saved her life. It's because Sunni's journal is now a pile of ash covering our chests and scattered across the tile.

Even though Sunni is gone, she just saved our lives.

Misty doesn't see it that way. "WHAT DID YOU JUST—?"

Another blast sears towards us, and Jia yanks us into her invisible world and out of harm's way. I shoot worried looks towards Wil, but he's holding his own. He's procured a blaster from a fallen hafelglob and climbed a rickety bookshelf, where he takes careful shots at the hafelglob closing in below.

Misty's ready to tear me a new one, but Jia shakes her arm violently. "Stop it. We're fighting for our lives here. Are you two all right?"

"Fine," I say. "I'm sorry, Misty."

"She's really gone now," she says quietly.

"Maybe it's for the best," Jia whispers. "It's better that her secrets are destroyed than in the hands of the Collective, right?"

Misty grits her teeth and nods slowly, but I know this is almost as terrible for her as the moment Sunni actually died.

"We need to get out of here. I'll take the left," she says, and dashes off.

"Wait for me!" Jia hisses, and as she catches up with Misty, she engulfs her in invisibility, leaving Wil and I defenceless.

He notices we've been abandoned and jumps down from the bookshelf. He's taken care of the hafelglob but I hear more slithering in the distance. Wil grabs my arm and we head towards the right. *They'll be fine. We have this blaster, and these.*

He points to our matching alien bands again. Mine feels cold against my overheating skin. It is not reassuring.

A guttural growl, a *SPLAT*, and a hafelglob rounds the corner. I stop short but Wil's still holding on to me. I wrench from his grip just as a mess of tentacles wrap around Wil's middle.

"Wil!"

A tentacle knocks his glasses and the ray gun to the floor. It doesn't matter. He squeezes his eyes shut. The hafelglob opens its mouth, revealing the rows of sharp teeth. Just as the alien lowers Wil into its cavern of doom, I run up and stomp on one of its stray, flailing tentacles. It grunts and tries to grab me but I avoid the flying tentacles with the skill of a highland dancer doing the sword dance.

Almost...got it... Even Wil's mind-voice is strained.

"Got what?" I shout.

The hafelglob screams in agony as it drops Wil. Its breath is a wave of rotten garbage and horrible body odour—I fall backwards onto the hard floor to avoid the stench. The tentacles slap the bookshelves, sending an avalanche of titles on top of us. I curl up into a little ball, praying that of all things, books won't be the thing giving me brain damage from this fight.

Ingrid. You still there?

Wil's voice gives me strength. I push my way out of the pile of books and find a battered and bruised Wil standing over the writhing hafelglob. Its screaming and belching won't allow us anonymity for long. We have to get out of here.

"What did you do?" I demand.

"I found its mind and filled it with horrible thoughts."

"Like what?"

"Its tentacles getting cut off, mostly."

I shiver. In the distance, I hear more sliming and Misty's ice balls shattering against wood and tile and, hopefully, slime.

Wil picks up the ray gun from the floor. "Maybe you should take this."

"Um..." I hug my chest. "I...I don't know..."

"You have to have something. Take it."

I reluctantly take it from his hands. It's heavier than I expect, and warm. Wil gestures to my wristband and I press the small blue button that activates the environment suit. A tingling sensation settles over my body as the liquid gel spreads from my arm and covers the rest of me, except for my eyes and mouth. It's a flexible body suit that tightly conceals everything about me, but it looks extremely awkward. I twist my lips in distaste, but at least I'm protected.

"Let's go," Wil says.

The bookshelves are almost as tall as the ceilings, and the dim eerie-green fluorescents cast long, disturbing shadows on the tile floor. I don't know where we're headed, but I hold the ray gun at eye level, afraid but ready to fire at the slightest sign of enemy movement.

I'm not sure what it is that makes me slow down. The cramp in my side is tolerable. There aren't any visible hafelglob around. We come to the end of our row. An intersecting narrow path lined with shelves crosses us, and beyond that are three more rows, all adjacent, that will probably lead us towards the fray. Misty and Jia are out of sight, but I hear Misty fighting off in the distance. I should really be heading towards her. But something in my mind clenches, as if an invisible hand is pulling on a clutch or pressing the brake pedal in my brain. My legs are made of molasses, and I'm sluggish, slowing down.

Wil seems to sense something is wrong and whips around. "What? Something wrong with your suit?"

I stop, holding up the ray gun, and swivel. My heart is beating a thousand times a minute, and my focus is razor sharp.

And then I see him through the bookshelves. Joseph G. Campbell. He's glowing, and then, he smiles at me. He's standing in the adjacent aisle.

I dash down the aisle but before I can reach the mysterious alien, he bursts silently into a million curly wisps of smoke. *Dammit.* I grasp at the smoke trails as they dissipate, and while I'm making a fool of myself, I accidently knock a book off the shelf. The *slap* it makes as it hits the floor echoes through the library, cutting through the shouts of the hafelglob near and far.

Wil hisses for me to be quiet as I bend to pick up the volume. It's too dim to see where it came from originally, so I'm about to shove it in with some other fifty-year-old books when I notice the tome's deckled edges. I press my hand against them, liking the feel, and slip a finger between the book's pages. The text is handwritten in a neat cursive—a handwriting that I've only seen once but would recognize anywhere.

"Oh my god," I whisper. "Wil."

His eyes dart cautiously around as he approaches my side to examine the tome. It is unmarked, bound with a thick cloth. It looks to be a hundred years old, at least, but the pages are so fragile that it could be even older. While checking for hafelglob, I open the book to the first page. Symbols that don't represent any Earth language greet me.

"This must be it," Wil whispers.

I blink, and suddenly the words reorder themselves. I almost drop the book in surprise. The title now reads: *Campbell's Multiple Verses. Volume II: A Discourse on the Origin of Life, also titled, Seeds of the Main Verse. Copied by Scribes in the False West, Before the Grounding.*

"Did you see that?" I hiss.

"Yeah," Wil replies. *We should get out of here now.*

"What about Jia and Misty?"

"We'll find them, if we can. Then, we're out." He gestures towards what I think is the east part of the restricted library, towards the noise of battle. "Just don't use that treatise as a shield, all right?"

A tinge of guilt lances my stomach. "Yeah, no, that's not going to happen, I promise."

I follow Wil once more into the heat of battle. I check my cell phone for the time: twenty to ten. We've been here longer than I thought. Although I've almost died a few times tonight, I am elated to have Joseph G. Campbell's actual writing against my chest. I was in need, and once again, he provided for me. He is working to protect me, and my friends. He is on our side.

Before us, the narrow rows widen, and a large shelf divides our path. Rapidly approaching hafelglob gurgle to the left.

Split up! Wil cries, shoving me to the right. *Meet me at the edge of campus. No one is guarding the door—we've got most of them. Use the band to get past the cameras and the security. You can make it.*

"But—"

No time to protest. He's gone, and there are three hafelglob going straight for him. He can handle them with his mental powers. I cannot.

But I'm not completely defenceless. Or that's what I whisper to myself as I race down the narrow pathway. The treatise is tucked safely under my arm. I hope the risk we've taken to retrieve it is worth it. I clamber through the rows of bookshelves, towards the exit.

Behind me, slime splatters against old books and well-walked tile as Wil fights his silent battle. Somewhere off to my right, Misty shouts curses at the aliens. A hafelglob passes me in the adjacent row, heading for Wil. I hold my breath, but the hafeglob has already heard me. I run faster, cursing my boots—they are giving away my position, and there's no time to stop and take them off.

I chance a glance over my shoulder. Now there are four hafelglob chasing me. They slime up the floors, secreting a sticky mucus that covers the tile, and they destroy any volume in their wake. I wonder if one of the hafelglob is Ohz. He would take any chance to see me this defenceless, to finally beat me down just as his mistress desires.

I'm almost to the exit. Once I'm out here, I still won't be free of the hafelglob, and each step forward is a hopeless reminder that escaping Sparkstone will not be easy without the Sparks to aid me. But I have to protect the treatise. Without it, I will have little hope of helping the students trapped here, and I will have little hope of helping myself.

It's darker by the exit, and in my desperation, I make a wrong turn. I run down an aisle that ends in a wall. I spin around to change my course, but the hafelglob stand alert seven feet away, blocking my only hope of escape. I point the ray gun at them and squeeze the trigger—nothing. The hafelglob advance, and I panic. I squeeze the trigger even harder and squeal as a blast of red energy bursts forth. It burns the top part of a bookshelf, sending books tumbling to the ground. Startled and frightened by its power, I drop the gun. I reach for it, but the hafelglobs' tentacles are longer and faster: they snatch it and now I am the target.

I back up against the wall and feel its cold embrace. I am done for.

Then, I see him. Again. Clearer than ever. The tall man with the ever-changing face. The air bends around him as he takes shape far down the aisle, behind the hafelglob.

"Campbell!" I shout.

The sound of my voice makes him more real. He steps through—but from where?—and the bookshelves and the floor shimmer and then burst as if they are made of a pliable, thick rubber. He stares at me, and smiles again, this mysterious man, whose facelessness is the definition of déjà vu.

Noticing Campbell's presence, the hafelglob spin and thrash their tentacles, sniffing him out.

"It is *he*," says one of the hafelglob.

But one of the slimy aliens cannot be distracted. I hear a voice I recognize, and all Ohz's tentacles flail in my direction. "Get the Crosskey! Do not let the Crosskey escape!"

My fingernails dig into my legs, and I squeeze my eyes shut. They must not get Joseph G. Campbell's treatise. The slimy residue of their bodies wraps around my arms and seeps into my environment suit. The wristband vibrates and the gel suddenly retracts, exposing me. "No, no, no, *leave me alone!*"

I shouldn't have come here tonight.

I should have gone to the concert with Ethan.

I am not going to die here tonight. I refuse.

They close in around me, and I feel a vacant, cold darkness. My ears pop, and I'm falling upward. Then, I find myself somewhere else.

CHAPTER 13

It's as if I've just blinked, and the Sparkstone Performance Centre now looms before me. The parking lot is small and it's full. A couple of people lean against the building, smoking. Through the glass doors, more people are huddled like sardines under the yellow fluorescents.

The concert. Ethan.

The book is cold under my arm, and it's raining slightly, enough to rinse some of the alien slime from my clothing. I look over my shoulder at the Sparkstone campus and then pull out my cell phone. Ten fifteen. Running from the hafelglob took five to ten minutes at most, so that means it took more than twenty minutes for me to get from the restricted library to the SPC.

And yet, it feels like no time has passed at all.

I walk cautiously towards the SPC entrance. The smokers give me a cursory glance, but no one stops me and asks if I have a ticket. It must be intermission, I realize as I step into a throng of excited people. There must be at least a hundred students here—far more people congregated here than I've seen since my arrival at Sparkstone, save for the people in the cafeteria. I strain and stand on my tippytoes to find Ethan, but it's pointless. I'm rammed and shoved as people make their way to a canteen selling chocolate bars and water at the far right. A set of double doors opposite me is closed. It must lead to the auditorium.

"...water is SO expensive. If you're going to serve drinks, why not juice or at least the *good* kinds of soda."

A loud, imposing voice rides over the sound of the crowd and impales my ears. *Kimberly.*

I follow her voice and there she is—with Ethan. His hands are shoved in his pockets, and he dutifully listens to her rant about the price of drinks in the venue. She's digging through her purse, a gargantuan leather thing that's twice the size of my face. Of course he'd give his extra ticket to her.

Jealousy leaves me when she happens to glance my way and does a double take. "Ingrid?" She waves enthusiastically and gestures for me to join them.

Ethan raises his eyebrows in surprise. I part my lips to apologize to him, but Kimberly grabs my hand and squeezes it excitedly.

"Did you just sneak in here?" she squeals.

"Oh um..." I glance back at the door. There's a beefy security guard standing there now, his arms folded. "I guess so."

Ethan smirks. He looks impressed. "I thought that you couldn't make it tonight."

"Um, change of plan!" I reply, a little too enthusiastically.

He points at Campbell's treatise. "You, uh, planning on reading during the concert?"

I hide it behind my back, as if that will help me. "Oh, no. I...I left in a hurry, forgot I even had it in my hand."

It's a stupid, flimsy excuse, but Kimberly's face lights up. "Oh, I've done that before! Once, back in high school, I took my paintbrushes to an English class because I'd pulled an all-nighter."

"Yes, but you're a scatterbrain," Ethan says.

She smiles and shrugs. "Say... if you want, I can take it back with me to the dorm. This music isn't really my jam anyway. I can just give it to you tomorrow, or whenever."

"Um..." Put Kimberly in danger? I couldn't do that, not when she's generously giving me the evening with Ethan. And not when this book could have all the answers I'm looking for. My eyes fall to her enormous bag. On the other hand...

"Just put it in your purse. It's raining and I don't want it to get wet."

"Of course, no problem."

I couldn't be more elated as I pass the tome to Kimberly. *The Collective will not expect this. It won't know where I am. It won't follow Kimberly because it doesn't know I'm at the concert, and oh god, I'm AT the concert with Ethan!* My thoughts become sober. *The Sparks. Wil did say that they've taken care of most of the hafelglob, and he can probably sense that I've made it out okay. I hope they're all right.*

She sticks it in her purse with the rest of her things, as if I haven't just risked life and limb for it, and quirks her eyebrows at Ethan. "Well. I should leave you two alone to... chat before the doors reopen."

Ethan gives her a playful shove, and she moves toward the door. She glances over her shoulder and winks at me. I'm surprised. Has Ethan told her something about me? Maybe about our kiss. Our time in the music room. Or worse, our fight.

I cross my arms and gather my courage. "Look, Ethan—"

He waves his hand. "Please. You don't have to apologize. I'm the one who's sorry. I...I really shouldn't have convinced you to sneak out, not when you had so much at stake."

My dad's life, I think, and picture him now, dying in a hospital. I can only pray that Jadore has not pulled his plug because I now hold Joseph G. Campbell's most important writings. But Ethan doesn't know about that. I play with the cell phone in my pocket, wondering if there's even any reception or service now so I can call my parents and tell them to run as far away as they can from civilization.

And then I realize what Ethan is actually referring to. "Oh. Right. Termination of my project," I say slowly. "I wasn't really worried about that much, to be honest. Jadore is really determined for me to finish it, since it's...well, I guess it's pretty important to her. So that's part of the reason I was willing to bend the rules."

"You mean you didn't bend the rules because of my rugged good looks?"

I blush. "Well...that may have been a contributing factor."

He steps closer to me. "I just don't want this stupid argument, and my stupidity, to affect our friendship. Or our...relationship."

Relationship. It's an untested word, with so many possibilities for us to discover. "I'm not mad at you. I was worried you hated me."

His voice is so low and serious I almost don't hear him over the crowd. "I could never hate you, Ingrid."

The people around us shift excitedly and start to move in one direction. I am held still by Ethan's intense gaze.

"The doors just reopened," Ethan says.

"Yeah, I see that."

"Do you want to go in or not?"

My heart leaps. Safety in numbers. Safety with Ethan. "Yes."

There's hope in his smile. "All right, then."

The crowd pushes us together, and even though the room is hot and smells musty, and there are quite a few people who don't know the meaning of hygiene, all that matters is that my shoulder is against Ethan's, and his hand is on the small of my back. Protecting me.

He says something to me but I can't hear him above the roar of the crowd.

"What?" I scream.

He tightens his grip on my arm and leans in to my ear. His breath is warm. "Don't get lost."

I grin at him. "I won't."

The band starts up again, and the crowd starts screaming. There are balcony seats above us, but most people are standing on the floor. Some form a mosh pit and dance without higher thought in the middle of a hundred strangers. Ethan claps and holds his hands high above us in the air, and hugs me close after each song. When a slower melody comes on, and the music vibrates in our cores, he closes his eyes, and I see him lose himself in the gentle downs and fierce ups of the tune. I lean my head on his shoulder and feel the colours pinging with the change of the chords, rejoicing when they match the blue and green mood lighting, humming in gentle discord when they don't, but always reacting, never stagnating.

After what feels like fifteen minutes but is surely an hour, the band wraps up their set, and the crowds scream for an encore. I'm shouting along with them, Ethan too. Our voices are hoarse but one. The band obliges and gives us two more songs. When the music stops for good, and my ears are ringing in the absence of sound, my feet squirm with discomfort, and I'm dying to sit down.

Ethan weaves us through the crowd until we're outside again. I'd almost forgotten what fresh air smelt like, and my lungs breathe it in greedily. I wriggle my toes in my boots and stand there, head up, eyes closed, happy to be alive for another day.

"You," Ethan says. "I wish I could paint you right now."

"Oh yeah?" I try not to move. "I guess you could take a picture."

"I think I will, if you don't mind."

"Go ahead."

I resist laughing and twitching as he fiddles with his phone. I only open my eyes when he says it's all right, and when I do, I see the stars reflected in his eyes.

"Do you want to see the photo?" he asks.

I shake my head. "Why don't you paint me, and then I can see how you see me."

His smile is mischievous. "Trying to get out of another modelling gig, I see, Miss Stanley."

"No!" I hit him playfully, but he catches my wrist and pulls me close.

"I'm glad you came," he says, and then kisses my forehead. Shivers run from that kiss down my face, down my legs, all the way to the tips of my toes.

You saved me, I say in my head. I cup his cheeks, feeling the day-old stubble, and bring his lips to mine.

"What is going on between us, Ingrid?" he whispers.

I can't even answer because he's kissing me back. He plants passionate pecks on my waiting lips, on my cheeks, and inhales my neck deeply. It's as if he can't get enough of me. I forget everything and laugh my satisfaction in his ear.

"Ethan, I want you." I don't recognize my own voice, but my heart knows it's mine.

He pulls back, caressing my shoulders. "I want to believe you."

"What do you mean?" The magic of his touch is fading. "I'm telling the truth."

His forehead heats mine as he presses against me. I feel his lips against mine as he speaks. "You seem to have trouble…keeping your commitments."

That's because I'm trying to fight an alien invasion!

"That's not who I am" is all I can say to that, because it's true. It's the only true thing I can say right now. I back away from his embrace. His warmth evaporates into the early fall night.

"I…I know. But—uh!" He slaps a hand to his temple and almost stumbles forward. I struggle to hold his weight up, but he pushes me gently away. He clutches his stomach and stumbles forward, groaning.

"What? What's wrong?" I kneel beside him, forcing him to look at me. In all of three seconds, his face is dripping with sweat, he's ghostly white, and his eyes are bloodshot and painfully blue.

"I…I don't know. I…ughhhh…"

I dig out my cell phone. "I'm calling 911."

But when I try, I find that reception has been cut off. Of course—Jadore didn't want me contacting my parents, and she didn't want the outside world to find out about the protest.

"I can't get through," I tell him, trying to keep the panic out of my voice. "Has this happened before?"

"I...no." He presses his forehead hard against the gravel. Small rocks dig into his skin. He grabs my head. "Don't...please don't leave me, Ingrid."

A crowd starts to form. Concerned onlookers ask if he's all right, if I'm responsible for him, and if they should call for help. I wave them off. If this is Spark-related, anything could happen, and if it's not, I refuse to let anyone see Ethan in this weakened state.

"I'm not leaving you," I tell him.

I grab his left arm and swing it over my shoulder. I'm a twig next to his built form, but dammit if I won't carry him back to his dorm. Teleportation would really come in handy *now,* but of course, when I want it, my mysterious power is nowhere to be found.

More concerned concert-goers ask if I need help, but Ethan seems to have found his feet and walks alongside me with my help. "Back to your room?" I ask.

"Yeah," he manages.

My shoulders burn with his weight but I bear the pain quietly and take it one step at a time. It's a twenty-minute walk back to campus, but it will probably take us double the time. I am thankful that the darkness shields us—I walk around the street lamps in case there are cameras attached to them. The last thing the Collective needs to see is us two potential Sparks hobbling along.

Ethan drips sweat as he walks but a bit of colour is returning to his cheeks. His breath is wheezy. I ask him a couple of questions to keep him with me, but he's slow to respond, and his voice is low and mumbling. I start to panic. If he falls unconscious, there's no way I can carry him.

I squeeze my eyes shut and concentrate. *I want to go to Ethan's room. Please, mysterious power, take me to Ethan's room.*

Nothing. I curse under my breath.

"Ingrid?"

I hear my name and freeze. It's dark and eerily quiet on the streets, save for Ethan's raspy breath and our slow, awkward footfalls.

"Who's there?" I hiss.

Jia materializes with Wil and Misty. I heave an excited sigh of relief. Ethan is too out of his mind to question where they've come from, and he does not object when Wil grabs his free arm and swings it over his shoulder. My back thanks him.

"What happened to him?" Jia asks.

"We were...talking, and then all of a sudden, he just...collapsed." Oh, and we were kissing. But I'm not going to tell them that part.

I think Wil senses that I'm not telling the whole truth, because he raises his eyebrows, but he doesn't pry, thank goodness. Ethan grunts and mutters something incomprehensible.

Jia relieves me of my position on Ethan's left side. "Where are we going?"

"His room," I say. "Wil, is there anything we can do for him?"

Wil touches the tips of his fingers to the side of Ethan's sweaty temple. "His brain. Something is going wrong in there. It's like...it's like his whole system is having a severe allergic reaction."

Is he allergic to me? We kissed—maybe some part of me is making him sick? No, that's silly. We kissed before and he didn't get sick.

"Ethan, did you eat any food in the cafeteria today?" I ask him.

But he's too far gone to answer. His head slumps against Wil's shoulder, and Jia balks under his weight. We're about ten minutes from his dorm, and between two street lamps.

"Can you use your power?" Jia asks.

"I tried. Nothing happened."

"Try again."

I nod and close my eyes, keeping a firm hand on Ethan. I visualize Morris House, even though I've never been inside. I try to think about what Ethan's room might look like.

And then, something *pings* inside me, and I feel as if my brain is suddenly in the in-between state, between sleep and wakefulness. But as soon as I realize this, I snap back to the present, and I'm still outside in the open with the Sparks.

"I can't." Frustration wells inside of me. "I *can't!*"

"It's all right," Wil says. His voice is soothing and calm. "Jia?"

She nods and touches my shoulder. "I'll make sure we get us there."

Misty takes my left hand, and I give her a small smile of thanks. It could be the darkness, but I think I see her return the smile.

Jia breathes in sharply, and in moments, cold, brisk reality dissolves into a fluid state of perpetual comfort. Every crunching step on the walkway is a small victory. Ethan drifts in and out of consciousness, and my whispers of hope and comfort to him come alive in light blue wisps of smoke that halo his ears and then evaporate. Jia is the personification of perseverance, never looking back. As we near Morris House, Wil is short of breath from carrying the brunt of Ethan's weight, but he does not complain. Nor does Misty make a sound.

They came back for me, when I needed it the most.

We use Ethan's key card, which we find in his pocket, to unlock the door. Then Wil wraps his hand around Ethan's and guides it to open the door so that the Collective will not know we've been here. We step through. There are two security guards at the desk, talking, and they drive fierce looks at the door that seems to open itself, but they go back to their conversation a few seconds later.

It's an agonizingly slow process, but we quietly go up the stairs, to the second floor, to Ethan's dorm room. My heart is louder than my breath. This is not how I imagined going to Ethan's dorm. He is not well, and I am in danger of being killed for my genes, and my friends are here, risking their lives for me. I am filled with adrenaline.

Again Wil uses Ethan's key card and opens the door with Ethan's hand. Ethan's room messy and unkempt, and smells a little like paint, but everything about the place is so him. Deep blue walls, a double bed pushed into the corner, and the smallest dresser I've ever seen—all sacrifices for the large space in the center of the room for three easels with paintings at various stages of completion.

As Wil and Jia carefully lay Ethan on the bed, Wil flicks his finger at the camera. *Once we go visible, I'll train the camera on the bed—it should only show Ethan as long as we stay out of the frame. I'll loop the feed, remove the audio, and cut and paste his image onto earlier timestamps in case someone bothers to check. It won't be a clean cover-up, but it may save us, and Ethan. All right?*

We nod, and when Jia gives us the okay, I let go of her, and Misty and I become visible. Ethan's head sinks into his pillow as Jia and Wil gently lay him down. His eyes open briefly, and he groans my name. Wil gives me a quick glance, and I purse my lips.

"It will be all right," I say to Ethan.

Now visible, Misty yanks her hand from mine, but the gesture is not mean—she's squinting at Ethan's paintings.

"Hey, Ingrid."

I join her beside an easel that's pointed away from the bed and the entrance, towards the bathroom.

The image is half-alive. A girl with red hair is playing the piano. She is a pencil-sketch skeleton, colour only in her flesh and her hair. The piano is detailed and wears a knot in its wooden side, and looking at the keys, I hear a faint whisper of a tune. Though it is a captured moment in time, frozen by the artist, the painting is so fluid that it looks as though it's moving.

The girl playing the piano can be no one else but me. A strand of curly red hair dangles in front of my face, which is not yet finished, as I look wistfully at the keys. There is something in the way that I'm drawn—the bold strokes that define my cheekbones, or the way my eyes are slightly hooded by my concentration—whatever it is, it's as if I'm looking at a more-than-perfect version of myself.

This is how he sees me. And he has captured me when I am most beautiful.

"Wow," Misty says, under her breath. She slides a glance over to me and says nothing more.

Jia and Wil are beside us, staring at the painting.

"I wonder what he'll do with this when he's finished," Jia whispers.

I twist my lip and look at Wil. He folds his arms. "Don't look at me. It's not my business. It's…a very nice painting of you, though."

I half-smile. "Thanks."

"If Jadore sees this, she's going to be pissed," Misty says.

"I don't think he'll let it leave the room," I say. "Surely he wouldn't paint this for an assignment."

"Let's not worry about that," Wil says. "What we should worry about is what to do with him."

"How is he?" I ask.

Wil looks grim. "I mean, he's still breathing. But he does not seem well. I hate to suggest it, but we should probably alert someone."

"Like Ms. Agailya?" I say. "She's his tutorial advisor."

"She's also part of the Collective," Misty says.

Jia looks worried. "Do you think he could die? Or…manifest a power?"

"I don't know," Wil says. "I mean, I never got sick, not that I can remember anyway, when I first started, you know." He taps the side of his shaven head. "But everyone is different."

"He can't die," I say firmly. I wring my shirt with both my hands. If I surrender him to the Collective, he may live—that is, if he's not a Spark and the Collective doesn't find his DNA useful enough to harvest. If I don't surrender him to the Collective, he might live a brief while before dying a potentially slow, painful death.

Ethan sits up suddenly, his eyes still closed, and starts coughing violently. His stomach heaves but nothing comes up. His T-shirt is wet with sweat. He's gasping for air, as if he's drowning.

"Ingrid," Wil says softly. "You know you have to."

I grab my hair and dig my fingernails into my scalp. I hate seeing him like this. But there's nothing I can do to help him. The aliens are the only ones who can figure out what's wrong.

They're also the ones who might kill him.

"Fine." I bite my nails. "Oh God, I hope this is the right thing to do. I hope we haven't just killed him."

Jia puts her arm around me. "It is better than leaving him here alone."

I try to take solace in her words, but as Ethan goes into another coughing fit, urgency surges through me. "Wil. How do we get a hold of Ms. Agailya? Or someone, without being suspicious?"

Wil massages his temples. "Okay. Ms. Agailya's not in her office."

"Does Ethan have her number on his cell phone? Do any of you have any of the professors' numbers?" I'm getting antsy.

"No. No number on his cell. And I definitely do not have any of the professors' numbers," Wil replies.

"One of us could go down and tell security," Jia says.

"But the Collective is looking for us!" I exclaim. "No. I won't allow us to create more lies and get into more trouble than we already are. And security, they could be regular humans for all we know. I..."

An idea hits me then, with a deep, powerful, black realization. I turn my eyes up to the camera. I know what I must do.

Wil catches my drift. "No, Ingrid. Too dangerous."

"Just me. I'll speak into the camera," I say. "Rest of you, back to your dorms."

Misty waves her icy finger. "No, no. We're not going to let you sacrifice yourself for him."

"Thanks, but this is my fault. Ethan is…he's my responsibility. You'd all do the same for someone you cared about." I look at Misty as I say this, and then at Jia. The three of them stand down.

"If I'm not here when you wake up tomorrow," I say, "the treatise is with Kimberly."

Wil raises his eyebrows, and Jia and Misty look as though they're about to protest, but I shake my head. "They're not going to suspect her, I don't think, so it was the safest move at the time." I look to Misty again. "I'm really sorry again about Sunni's journal."

Misty nods slowly, trying to hold back the emotion from her face.

I gesture to the camera. "Wil, can you make the camera normal again?"

Jia beelines for the door. Before Wil changes the camera, Misty marches up to me and squeezes my arms—the closest thing she can manage to a hug. One hand is warm and the other cold, but they are both filled with feeling, and that is all I can ask of her.

"I don't agree with this," she mutters. "But at least your death might mean somethin'."

Death. I don't want to think about it like that. Ethan dry-heaves again and curls into the fetal position. He's moaning and talking in tongues, and his skin is even whiter than before.

She releases me and joins Jia at the door. Wil swirls his finger at the camera just as Jia grabs his arm. "Good luck,

Ingrid," he says, before he disappears, and the door shuts behind their invisible bodies.

I kneel before Ethan. His flesh is clammy and cold, and when I touch him, he flinches violently and cries out. I rise to my feet and stare at the harsh red light. I clench my fists. I refuse to be afraid.

"This is Ingrid Louise Stanley. I am the Crosskey. Please, if you're from the Collective, come to Ethan Millar's room now. Something is horribly wrong with him. You can do whatever you want with me. Just for the love of everything I care about—*save him.*"

CHAPTER 14

Less than two minutes later, the aliens show up.

Neither Ms. Agailya nor Professor Jadore is among the four who arrive. They're dressed in blue scrubs and all of them wear white lab coats, and they certainly look like humans, but there is something unhuman about the way they barge into the room, not acknowledging my presence, and immediately begin poking and prodding Ethan.

I stand by one of the easels, arms crossed, treating each breath as if it's my last. The minutes stretch into forever as the medical team takes Ethan's blood sample, inject him with a clear liquid, and lay wet cloths on his forehead. They speak to him in soothing tones, and eventually his desperate moans become gentle murmurs and he seems to stabilize.

Finally, one of the medics seems to notice I exist. He approaches me and bows his head, and speaks in a heavy Latin-language accent. "Ingrid Louise Stanley. Please come with me now."

"Will Ethan be all right?"

"He will be fine. Please come with us, now."

I nod and follow the man in scrubs out of Ethan's room and down the stairs. He shows his badge to security, and the two men at the desk give me confused looks, but they don't ask any questions.

I prepare to be taken to the secret hangar bay in Conrod Building, but to my surprise, we head back towards Rita House. "Are we—?"

Something on the man's belt beeps, and he pulls out a walkie-talkie. The person on the other end sounds female, but her words are full of static and jumbled.

"Acknowledged," the man says, and replaces the device on his belt. He looks at me with regret in his eyes. "I apologize, Crosskey. This may hurt."

"What may—?"

His movement is fluid and fast. I feel a stabbing sensation in the back of my neck. My eyes roll into the back of head. I'm lightweight, and finally free.

∼✑

When I open my eyes, I'm back in my bed in my dorm room. The sunlight coming through the large windows has warmed the room to an uncomfortable temperature. I stumble halfway to the bathroom before realizing that I am, yet again, not dead.

"A certain someone must be watching out for me. That or I am very lucky," I mutter as I step onto the heated bathroom tile. Someone removed my boots. I check the front door. Yep, they're there, neatly placed. The socks on my feet are not the ones I was wearing yesterday.

I flick on the lights over the sink and inspect my body. My hair is not frizzy from hours of sleep. It looks as if it has been washed and styled. The clothes I'm wearing—silky pajamas, in a brilliant blue—they're not mine. Even my face feels and looks radiant, and my eyebrows have been plucked as well.

"What the ... ?" I frown at myself, but my reflection has no answers. She can only show me the truth.

I march out of the bathroom and throw my hands up at the black circle of a camera above my bed. "So, I don't know what you did to me while I was sleeping but ... but I'm keeping the pajamas."

The red light blinks once. I don't know if that's good or bad, but whoever is on the other end has heard me.

Ethan. His name floods me with fear as last night's events surge into my mind. "You better not have hurt him."

The light does not blink.

I check the alarm clock. Jesus, it's almost noon. I double check my phone. It's Saturday. But crap. We still have that extra tutorial ... and it starts in forty-five minutes. Not as if this really matters, not with all I've been through in the past twenty-four hours. Maybe members of the Collective are on their way here now to take me away. Regardless, I have to find Ethan. I have to know if he's alive.

I'm about to fly out the door when a familiar *beep-boop-beep* sound comes from under my bed. A video message?

I frantically retrieve my laptop from its hiding spot and pull open the top. It only takes a second to boot up, and sure enough, I'm receiving a video call—from my parents. My hand shakes as I press the answer button.

The mouse spins as it loads the stream, and both my mother and my father appear. Dad is sitting in his favourite armchair, in the living room, with a blanket over his knees. Mum mutters and adjusts the camera, and then perches on the arm of the chair. Dad tells her to stop fiddling with the camera, that it's fine, and to stop worrying.

I don't think I've ever been more relieved to see them in my life.

"Dad! Mum!" I cry, pressing my face against the screen. "You're...you're..."

"Yes, we're home!" Mum says. "Did we catch you at a bad time? About to go to class?"

I dismiss that thought with a wave. "Not yet, no. Mum—"

"Your hair looks very pretty today!"

I run my hand over it. "Yeah, thanks."

"New style? I like it!"

"Yeah...yeah, thanks. Dad, are you okay? What happened? Aren't you still—?"

Dad chuckles at my concern and runs his hand over his chest. "I'm fine, Ingrid. See? Good as new."

"What happened?"

"Well..." Mum glances with concern at my unconcerned father. "After I got off the phone with you, he was taken to the hospital. The doctors did everything they could, but his injuries only seemed to be getting worse. It was like he was having an allergic reaction to any painkillers they were giving him. Honestly." She shakes her head. "I kept trying to tell those doctors, try some other drug, I don't care if it's experimental or approved by the FDA or whomever. His life depended on it. Most of the doctors seemed to ignore me, but finally, two days ago, the word must have gotten through that we were desperate to try anything experimental. So with your father unconscious, I consented to an experimental trial of a new drug they're developing at the University of British Columbia.

Wasn't covered by insurance, of course. Had to pay out of pocket." Dad grimaces, but she continues. "I was worried last night. I tried to call you, but I couldn't get through. Where were you?"

"The...cell phone lines must have been down."

She doesn't question whether or not cell phone lines are real. "It was bad, Ingrid. Very bad."

"But...but the drug worked?"

"Oh yes, it did," Dad says. "I woke up this morning feeling better than ever."

I frown and glance up at the camera, then back to the alarm clock. Still have a bit of time. "Yeah, me too. I...I was really worried, Dad. I'm really glad you're okay."

"Yes, so are we!" Mum exclaims, squeezing Dad's shoulders, pulling him into a side hug. "And I'm sorry I couldn't come get you, Ingrid. Did you still need me to?"

It's so tempting. More than anything I want to say yes.

"I...don't think I can leave just yet," I say quietly.

"No, I wouldn't want you to," Dad replies. "You study hard, work on your projects. Focus on that and we'll come visit soon."

I swallow a lump in my throat. "Okay, Dad."

"We should let her go now," Dad says, mostly to Mum.

She looks disappointed. "Oh! Don't you have more time? It is a Saturday."

"Well, actually, I do have an extra tutorial today, and I just need to go find someone before that tutorial starts."

"Someone? Who?" Mum asks. "It isn't some boy, is it?"

I roll my eyes but my cheeks heat, and my cheeks cannot lie.

"Listen to your father and concentrate on your studies,"

Mum says. "But maybe one day this week we can catch up and you can tell me all about him."

I purse my lips. "Okay, Mum. Love you."

"We love you too, Ingrid. Very much. Have a good day."

"You too. Don't work too hard, Dad."

"Oh, I've got some time off. Your mother's not letting me leave this chair."

"Good." I nod emphatically. "That's good."

"Goodbye, then," Dad says. "Good luck with your studies."

"Bye, Dad. Bye, Mum."

I hover over the end call button because I really, really don't want it to end. I'm scared that if I hang up, I might never see them again, that Jadore is playing a nasty trick on me and will send Collective agents to kill my parents the moment I turn off the screen. Mum and Dad wave goodbye until Mum starts fiddling with their laptop and Dad goes back to scolding her about not knowing how to work the software. Then midsentence, in a blink, they're gone.

I stare at the blank screen for a good five minutes. Devastated. But also exhilarated. My dad is okay. I'm still super far away from them, but my parents are okay. Thanks to some mysterious drug. No doubt the Collective had a hand in that—but why?

Just because my parents are okay doesn't mean Ethan is.

I don't bother showering as I don't want to ruin my seemingly alien makeover. A disturbing theory crosses my mind: *What if the Collective dresses up its victims before they're slaughtered, to lure them into a false sense of security?* I try not to think about it. I look better than I've looked in weeks, and this makes me feel confident. *I will find you, Ethan, and if you are dead, the Collective will pay.*

After I'm dressed in a fresh skirt and a T-shirt that hangs off my shoulders, I pull on my boots and run out of the building. I text Ethan's phone, cursing every second that he does not respond. With thirty minutes until tutorial starts, I run to Morris House. The man at the security desk gives me a dubious look when I tell him that I have to know if Ethan is in his room. I don't know whether he's part of the Collective or just a random human, but he rings Ethan's room. No answer.

I'm desperate. Fifteen minutes until tutorial. I race to the Lewis Art Building. The same girl who met me before is at the desk, and I ask her if Ethan has come by while I check my phone for messages. No new messages, and Ethan has not been at the studio today.

Leaving the art studio building, I concentrate on Wil, letting him know that I'm still alive. I hope he can hear my thoughts. I dig my cell phone out, knowing I've received no response. Time, once again, is not my friend. I have to get to tutorial and face Jadore.

Dread fills me the closer I get to MacLeod Hall. I feel as though I'm abandoning Ethan, committing adultery with each pace. I try to tell myself that I will find him, that if he does not reply within five minutes I will barge into President Dean's office and demand to know if he has been transferred.

I swing open the MacLeod Hall door. Ms. Agailya hovers in the lobby. Her face lights up when she sees me. "Ingrid."

Reluctantly, I stop. "Where's—?"

And then I see him. He appears in the doorway of one of the classrooms, with Kimberly. She makes a funny face and he cracks up. My heart leaps. He's alive. And he looks fine. Never better. His cheeks are flush with colour, and his hair is styled, and he's wearing a pair of brand-new jeans and a long-sleeved black shirt.

"Ethan," I say under my breath, and start towards him.

Ms. Agailya floats in front of me, blocking my view. "One moment, Ingrid."

I'm antsy. I have to talk to him. What if he remembers being invisible last night? What if he's forgotten about the concert, our kiss? I clench my hands and stare defiantly at Ms. Agailya.

"I know you are anxious to speak with him," she says. Her voice is especially melodic today, and something in it is deliberately soothing. The tension in my shoulders seems to melt as she speaks. "Your actions last night were risky. They put not only your life in danger, but the lives of your friends as well. We know your faces. We know your DNA. We *know* you have ripened, Ingrid. But..." She hesitates. "The council voted. You and your friends will live to see more days yet."

"Why are you telling me this?" I ask, lowering my voice. "I thought—"

"Remember what I told you."

I think to our earlier conversation with ease. Her hand on my shoulder, it's making my brain work at double its regular speed. Her words return: *The Collective is not one mind.*

"How are we still alive?" I ask instead.

Ms. Agailya steps to the side. Kimberly has gone, and Ethan is leaning against the wall, texting. He's smiling.

"You saved him," Ms. Agailya says simply. "And for your kindness, I pleaded your case before the council.

You are safe, Ingrid, for now, so long as you keep yourself out of trouble."

I frown. "So Ethan—what was wrong with him?"

"You will be late for tutorial. Professor Jadore is not in a good mood today," Ms. Agailya replies as she continues down the hallway. "And I thank you for your good deed. I trust you have found that it has been repaid."

As she leaves me, I stand in stunned silence. I run my hands through my treated hair and I think about her repayment for my "good deed"—my dad's life, along with my life. Ethan is important to the Collective. Perhaps even more important than I am. Whatever Ms. Agailya is doing at Sparkstone, her *research*, it directly concerns Ethan. That means he will be safe so long as Ms. Agailya's research is important to the Collective. But as soon as it isn't…

We are all in a rat maze. But at least I'm not alone.

Ethan looks up from his phone, and our eyes meet. His smile grows to a grin. "Hey, you. I was just texting you back. You look…positively radiant."

I race towards him, throw my arms around his neck, and squeeze him as tight as I can, praying that I will never see the moment when I have to let go.

EPILOGUE

Jadore is watching the horizon, waiting for the dreadfully poisonous sun to rise and threaten her fragile non-human eyes. Then the office temperature—kept at a balmy forty degrees Celsius at night when the students are not around—drops. She shivers and rubs her human skin, thinking about the cream in her drawer. It is almost time to apply it.

After Campbell leaves.

He is standing behind her, after all. How long he has been there, she doesn't know. Now that he has returned, she will have to get used him popping in and out of rooms again—never really appearing or disappearing, but rather, just *being*, as if he always existed in the moment.

She gathers her courage, courage that she treasures and now has a name for, and spins around to face him. "You have returned."

"I was summoned."

"The Crosskey." Of course. Her display in the cafeteria. Or perhaps it was the trick she pulled in the underground warehouse. Either case, she brought him fully into this world, from wherever he had been hiding or trapped before. And the girl had failed to tell her the secrets she knew about the mysterious, ancient being.

His form has stabilized. Human, of course. This is not a surprise, given his fondness for the creatures. A young middle-aged man with light hair. His long overcoat hides a dress shirt and dress pants. He saunters forward, his boots barely a whisper on the floor.

"Her pull was strong. Stronger than I expected," he says. "I thought I would not get through. To be trapped in the between-space—in some ways it's better than being *here*..." He clears his throat. "But that is inconsequential. What matters is I have arrived and am ready to resume my duties."

I bet you are, Jadore thinks bitterly. "I have been anticipating your arrival. You were away for quite some time."

"That, I cannot control. I am the Other, the Twenty-Seventh. The End, but never the Beginning. But this does not mean that my ability to travel is limitless."

Whenever Campbell sputters off whatever other names he's given himself, it gives her a headache. A sentient being should only have one or two names at most. Anything more becomes a pain to remember. This preference, however, could be a remnant desire from her early days as a non-sentient being in the swamps.

Jadore gets right to the point. There is no use feigning small talk with Campbell. "The Crosskey has revealed her power."

Campbell looks only mildly surprised. "I...I saw this...yes, seconds ago."

"Days, Campbell. It is days for us." She hates the way he cannot keep track of time, here, in the regular world. "She is strong. And she has ripened. We can harvest her any day now."

"But you won't."

"This is what you want. You *need* her."

Campbell's face, for a brief moment, reflects a tortured side that Jadore rarely sees. "I do need her," he says quietly. "But she is not ready yet. The others are not yet ready. Phase four is still a ways off."

"We could accelerate the schedule."

Yes, anything to get rid of this sorry bastard. Once the Collective is free of his influence, I can get on with my own harvesting plans.

"Time." Campbell shoves his hands into his pockets and faces the window. "Her presence is a constant reminder of the mistakes my people have made."

More cryptic nonsense. It is best to ignore it. "I will draft a vote for the council. We will decide tomorrow whether to go ahead with the acceleration. Can I count on your support?"

"Hmm? Support, Ja'Dor'Esss?" He pronounces her name, her real, given name, with the grace and precision of a native tongue. It is a string of words that was created for her people, when the Collective brought them out of the swamps and into the stars.

"Yes, Campbell. Will you support the acceleration to phase four, or is that schedule too ambitious for your tastes?"

The man looks conflicted. *Conflicted is better than staunchly opposed.*

"She has shown herself to me," he says quietly. He

absently strokes the bookshelf. "Her voice is sweeter than…sweeter than I have ever a right to know. The power within her has awakened, but she has no control. Phase four is one thing. But for phase five, we need that control. Without the stability—"

"There are ways to accelerate her control. If we could extract her from this environment—"

"I won't allow that."

He is decisive this time. He blurs as he moves towards her, and then his face is before hers. A perfect sculpture of a humanoid man. To be that perfect, Jadore would need more cream, more surgery. The human DNA swirling within her urges her to lean in, to touch her lips to his lips, to act like the slobbering young humans on campus.

Disgusting. She turns her cheek.

Campbell can see her arousal, she knows. He sees everything. His lips turn upward; he is amused. Jadore is no longer in control of this interaction. She allowed his charm and his experience to cloud her judgement.

"Out of my office. *Now.*" She flicks her tongue at him, and though her cheeks are flushed with blood, showing tongue is not considered a sexual act within her species. It is a warning. A taste of the air, to sense the intruder's strength. *Leave my territory or be eaten.* Her fingers tingle with electricity, power bestowed upon her by the Collective.

By *him.*

He chuckles and backs away. But his gaze does not leave her. "I admire your ambition, Ja'Dor'Ess. Truly, I do." And then just as quickly as he came to her, he is at the door, and his face is no longer the incarnation of beauty. A dark cloud hovers in his expression. His expression is difficult to see now that he is at the door, and his form is enveloped in the invading sunlight, but another flick of her forked tongue tells her everything she needs to know. He is not afraid of her. He is angry. Heat rolls off him in waves, and although the Collective built her to fight, she is a blade of grass next to this ancient being whose age and experience eclipses the universe itself.

"I have no issues with you pulling strings behind my back. I enjoy the challenge of guessing what you will do next. You have the authority to do whatever it takes to see us to phase five. But if you *ever*"—the heat is almost unbearable, and if Jadore were in her native skin, she would've sought the comforting muds by now—"stunt the Crosskey's voice, harm her ability to sing, her ability to reach out to another in a time of need again, I will erase your existence."

Jadore draws in a breath of hot air. "You are threatening me, Campbell? You *need* me if you ever want to see your precious race again."

He opens the door. "I may need your assistance in some matters. But in seeing my race? I left them long ago, when the entirety of existence was a child. That is not the reason I am here. It is not the driving force behind the Sparkstone Project."

"Then why are you here? You pop in and out of the council's business as if you are entitled to do so. I am in charge of this project!" Sparks fly from her fingers and hit the tile, where they fizzle out. "I will decide what forces drive us forward."

Campbell's form flickers. He is fading away, but his voice is omnipresent in the room, and in her head. "Tread carefully, my pet. I will shut down this operation if you stray too far from its mission statement. There is only one thing that matters to me, and to the continued existence of intelligent beings everywhere. One thing only: I must save *her*."

Join Ingrid, Misty, Wil, and Jia as they continue to battle the Collective and discover Campbell's secret agenda in:

BOOK THREE
THE SPARKSTONE SAGA

Acknowledgements

Although Sir Copy Right was smitten with the Acknowledgements Faery and was ready to fight for her, he did not feel it was right to insert himself randomly into the middle of stories, as the faery was doing.

After hours of negotiating with publishers on the Acknowledgement Faery's behalf with no success, Sir Copy Right devised his own plan. He began placing acknowledgements on the copyright pages of books. However, acknowledgements can run long, and once publishers caught wind of what Sir Copy Right was doing, they started cutting copyright pages altogether! This only made the Acknowledgements Faery more angry . . .

What will happen to the Acknowledgements Faery and Sir Copy Right next? I don't know, you'll have to read my next book to find out!

Champions of the Acknowledgements Page:

Mum, Dad, Jessie & family, Marie & Joe, Sam (for always being there), Twitter friends (many #wordsprings contributed to the making of this book), my social media followers, and everyone who chats with me at my table during the conventions around the country. Thank you for your support!
And Dave, always.

About the Author

Clare C. Marshall grew up in rural Nova Scotia with very little television and dial up internet, and yet, she turned out okay. She has a combined honours degree in journalism and psychology from the University of King's College, and is a graduate from Humber College's Creative Book Publishing Program. She is a full-time freelance editor, book designer, and web manager and has clients all over the world. When she's not writing, she enjoys playing the fiddle and making silly noises at cats.

*Photo Credit:
Terence Yung*

Facebook: Facebook.com/faeryinkpress

Twitter: @ClareMarshall13
@FaeryInkPress

Website: FaeryInkPress.com

If you enjoyed this book, please consider writing a review on Amazon or on Goodreads. Thank you!

STARS IN HER EYES
Sparkstone Saga #1
by Clare C. Marshall

$13.95
165 pages

YA Science Fiction
Ages 12+
ISBN: 9780987779489

Burn hot and cold. Read minds. Disappear at will. Dream your own death. Welcome to Sparkstone University, where some students are more gifted than others.

When Ingrid learns she's been accepted at the hyper-secretive Sparkstone University, she is sceptical. It's an honour to attend, apparently, and yet barely anyone has ever heard of the place.

And everyone seems a little too happy that she's there: especially when she meets Sunni and her group of friends. They seem to already know Ingrid. As if she was expected. Expected to save Earth from an imminent alien invasion. Like she has superpowers or something.

As if magic and mutations exist. As if aliens are really planning to attack.

That just sounds ridiculous. There's no such thing.

...right?

Wrong.

THE VIOLET FOX
The Violet Fox Series #1
by Clare C. Marshall
$20.95
288 pages

YA Fantasy/Adventure
Ages 12+
ISBN: 9780987779441

Run.
That's what instinct told me.
But to save the secrets of my people
and to protect my brother
I have to become the enemy.

There are two kinds of people in the land of Marlenia. The Marlenians, who live on the surface, and the Freetors, who are forced to live underground.

The war between them ended two hundred years ago, but the Freetors still fight for the right to live under the sun. Fifteen-year-old Kiera Driscoll embodies the Freetors' hopes as the Violet Fox. In a violet cape and mask, she sneaks around Marlenia City stealing food and freeing her people from slavery.

Then the Elders task her with a secret mission: retrieve a stolen tome that contains the secrets of Freetor magic, something the Marlenians both fear and covet. Kiera must disguise herself as a noblewoman and infiltrate the Marlenian castle before the Freetor-hating Advisor finds out her real identity, before her brother is imprisoned because of the secrets he hides, and before she falls any more in love with the prince she's supposed to hate.

More is happening in the castle than she realizes, and Kiera is faced with a difficult choice. Will she be loyal to her people and their fight for freedom, or will she be loyal to her heart?

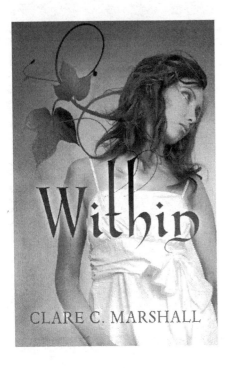

WITHIN
by Clare C. Marshall

$11.99
192 pages

YA Supernatural/Thriller
Ages 16+
ISBN: 9780987779403

Trinity Hartell's life changed after the accident. Left with irreversible brain damage, she becomes a burden to her mother, a cause for heartbreak for her boyfriend Zack, and a flattened obstacle for her jealous best friend, Ellie.

But then she starts writing. Perhaps it's a coincidence that the psychotic, murderous protagonist of her novel bears a striking similarity to the charming Wiley Dalton, a mayoral candidate in the upcoming election.

Or, perhaps not...

54865058R00151

Made in the USA
Charleston, SC
15 April 2016